W9-BYL-089

Harlan wanted her to be his wife!

What was she going to do? What did she *want* to do?

"Rose?"

She heard him coming up behind her. Quickly she sucked in several breaths of cool night air.

His fingers touched the back of her neck and she wilted inside.

"I know this is very sudden for you," he murmured. "But please don't say no."

Her throat grew tighter. "Just what sort of marriage would this be?"

"What do you mean?"

She glanced over her shoulder at him. He was such a strong, handsome man. A man made to love a woman. He didn't need her for a wife. He needed someone who would be not only a companion and friend, but also his lover. If he didn't realize that, she certainly did.

"I mean—" Oh, how could she do this? She turned to face him. "Are you expecting us...to have a sexual relationship?"

Dear Reader,

Love is always in the air at Silhouette Romance. But this month, it might take a while for the characters of May's stunning lineup to figure that out! Here's what some of them have to say:

"I've just found out the birth mother of my son is back in town. What's a protective single dad to do?"—FABULOUS FATHER Jared O'Neal in Anne Peters's *My Baby, Your Son*

"What was I thinking, inviting a perfect—albeit beautiful—stranger to stay at my house?"—member of THE SINGLE DADDY CLUB, Reece Newton, from *Beauty and the Bachelor Dad* by Donna Clayton

"I've got one last chance to keep my ranch but it means agreeing to marry a man I hardly know!"—Rose Murdock from *The Rancher's Bride* by Stella Bagwell, part of her TWINS ON THE DOORSTEP miniseries

"Would you believe my little white lie of a fiancé just showed up—and he's better than I ever imagined!" —Ellen Rhoades, one of our SURPRISE BRIDES in Myrna Mackenzie's *The Secret Groom*

"I will not allow my search for a bride to be waylaid by that attractive, but totally unsuitable, redhead again!"—sexy rancher Rafe McMasters in *Cowboy Seeks Perfect Wife* by Linda Lewis

"We know Sabrina would be the perfect mom for us—we just have to convince Dad to marry her!"—the precocious twins from Gayle Kaye's *Daddyhood*

Happy Reading!

Melissa Senate
Senior Editor

Please address questions and book requests to:
Silhouette Reader Service
U.S.: 3010 Walden Ave., P.O. Box 1325, Buffalo, NY 14269
Canadian: P.O. Box 609, Fort Erie, Ont. L2A 5X3

THE RANCHER'S BRIDE

Stella Bagwell

Silhouette

R O M A N C E™

Published by Silhouette Books

America's Publisher of Contemporary Romance

To Charles and Denise,
for their appreciation of the great West
and its cowboys.
Love ya.

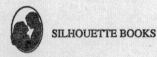 SILHOUETTE BOOKS

ISBN 0-373-19224-X

THE RANCHER'S BRIDE

Copyright © 1997 by Stella Bagwell

Books by Stella Bagwell

Silhouette Romance

Golden Glory #469
Moonlight Bandit #485
A Mist on the Mountain #510
Madeleine's Song #543
The Outsider #560
The New Kid in Town #587
Cactus Rose #621
Hillbilly Heart #634
Teach Me #657
The White Night #674
No Horsing Around #699
That Southern Touch #723
Gentle as a Lamb #748
A Practical Man #789
Precious Pretender #812
Done to Perfection #836
Rodeo Rider #878
*Their First Thanksgiving #903
*The Best Christmas Ever #909
*New Year's Baby #915
Hero in Disguise #954
Corporate Cowgirl #991
Daniel's Daddy #1020
A Cowboy for Christmas #1052
Daddy Lessons #1085
Wanted: Wife #1140
†The Sheriff's Son #1218
†The Rancher's Bride #1224

Silhouette Special Edition

Found:
One Runaway Bride #1049

**Heartland Holidays Trilogy
†Twins on the Doorstep

STELLA BAGWELL

lives in the rural mountains of southeastern Oklahoma, where she enjoys the wildlife and hikes in the woods with her husband. She has a son, a wonderful daughter-in-law and a great passion for writing romances—a job she hopes to keep for a long time to come. Many of Stella's books have been transcribed to audiotapes for the Oklahoma Library for the Blind. She hopes her blind audience, and all her readers, will continue to enjoy her stories.

Daddy—

Much as I love you, sometimes I really miss my mom. And now that I'm almost a teenager, I need to talk to her about some things—things that I _really_ don't want to talk to you about! And so I've been thinking. Rose is a really nice lady. She's friendly and she's really pretty when she smiles. She likes me, I think, and she's teaching me to cook real food. She's even going to let me baby-sit the twins! So since she is spending so much time with us, I was wondering if you're interested in marrying her.

Pretty please?

Love,

Emily

Chapter One

Rose Murdock reined the sorrel alongside the fence and stared in shocked dismay. Each of the six strands of barbed wire had been cut, then carefully twisted back together.

Quickly, she stepped down from the saddle and examined the ground on both sides of the fence. The soil was crusty and dry from a drastic lack of rain. Even so, Rose managed to pick up the faint marks of hoof tracks. Too many to count!

Leading the sorrel, called Pie, behind her, she followed the tracks down a long slope of land until she reached the river. The hoof prints stopped at the watering hole, then turned and headed back the way she'd come from the cut wire.

Someone had cut the fence to water their cattle on Bar M land! Who would have done such a thing, then fixed the fence neatly back in place? The cattle were obviously not on her land now. She'd ridden out this whole pasture today and not seen one stray.

Sighing, Rose pushed the gray cowboy hat off her head.

Its stampede string caught at the front of her neck, preventing the hat from falling further than the middle of her back.

Sweat glistened on the soft features of her face. She mopped it away with the back of her denim sleeve, then carefully scanned the horizon to the east.

Across the barbed wire fence lay Harlan Hamilton's ranch, the Flying H. From what she could read of the tracks, the cattle had come from that direction. But she couldn't imagine the man doing such a thing without notifying her or her sisters first. Open range in New Mexico had come to an end a long time ago. No one with any courtesy or respect would drive their cattle onto another rancher's land without asking permission first.

But then, she didn't really know Harlan Hamilton. At least, not personally. She'd seen him maybe three separate times, the last being almost a year ago when he'd stopped by the ranch to visit her late father, Tomas.

The two of them had been friends and Tomas had spoken highly of Harlan. Yet Rose had never done more than say a polite hello to the man. Not because she had anything against the rancher next door. Saying hello was as far as she went with any man.

Well, it looked as though more than a simple greeting was going to have to be said to him now, she decided. And unfortunately it looked as though she'd been picked for the job.

Rose mounted Pie and turned him in a northerly direction. For three miles or more she rode along the fence line until she reached two rock pillars flanking a metal gate. At the top of one pillar, the words Flying H Ranch were etched in black iron.

The gate didn't appear to be locked so she opened it, led her horse through, then carefully closed it behind her. Back on Pie, Rose rode steadily down the dirt road that cut through the desert hills east of Hondo. Knee-high sage and piñon pine grew on either side of her. Now and then a choya stood in bloom, though she didn't see how the plants were managing to survive, much less bloom in this drought that had lasted more than two months now.

As the horse trotted on, Rose grew more nervous. She'd already been sweating from the afternoon heat, but in the past few minutes, her hands had become slick with perspiration and her mouth was as dry as the fine dust stirred by the horse's hooves.

She didn't relish exchanging words with Harlan Hamilton. She wasn't good around men. Not like her sister Justine, who'd just married the local sheriff. Nor was she like her younger sister, Chloe, who wasn't afraid to look a man in the eye and speak her mind.

But Justine wasn't here to do her talking for her and Chloe was back at the ranch with hardly enough time in the day to work the horses and take care of the twins.

No, she couldn't ask either of her sisters to do this for her, Rose thought with grim determination. Since her father had died and money had grown tight, the cattle had become her responsibility. It was her job to confront trespassers, whomever they might be.

More than two more miles passed before Rose spotted the house in the distance. Like her own home, it was structured in stucco and sat wedged between a row of ragged poplars and a stand of piñon pine.

As Rose rode closer, she could see the place was neither large nor elaborate. The house needed painting and, other than the scrubby trees casting a few spots of flimsy shade, there were no flowers or grass or fence to declare a dividing line between yard and pasture.

Pie didn't have to be tethered to stay put. Rose left him a few yards away from the house and walked slowly toward the porch. Through the screen door she could hear the sound of a television playing.

She was climbing the steps when a girl of twelve or thirteen opened the door and stepped onto the concrete porch. Her straight blond hair was pulled back into a sloppy ponytail. Cutoff blue jeans covered part of her long, coltish legs; the rest of her thin adolescent figure was hidden beneath an oversize T-shirt. She looked at Rose as if visitors were an odd commodity on the Flying H.

"Hello," Rose said. "Is Mr. Hamilton home?"

The girl gave a single nod of her head. "Daddy's down at the barn."

"Would it be all right if I walked down there to see him?"

The girl shrugged. "Suit yourself."

Rose turned to go, then a thought struck her and she looked back at the sullen teenager. "If your mother is in the house, she might be able to help me."

"I don't have a mother," she said curtly, then went back into the house before Rose could make any sort of reply.

What a sad little girl, Rose thought. She hadn't known that Harlan Hamilton had a child or that he was single. How long had he been without a wife and his daughter without a mother? she wondered.

As Rose approached the barn, she spotted the owner of the Flying H trying to coax a black yearling to follow a lead rope. The young horse was balking. Each time the man tugged on the rope, the animal stiffened its front legs and reared its head back.

Still unnoticed, Rose walked up to the wooden corral and stood quietly watching. Her neighbor was a big man. At least two inches past six feet, and she figured he weighed well over two hundred pounds. Faded jeans clung to his long strong legs and a gray chambray work shirt was stretched taut across his broad shoulders. He had a lean waist and large, menacing arms. Dark, almost black hair waved from beneath the straw cowboy hat on his head.

Normally Rose didn't notice men in the physical sense. She had long ago lost her appetite for sex or romance, and what a man did or didn't look like hardly mattered to her. But something about this man was urging her to take a closer look than usual.

The sight of a woman, a beautiful one at that, standing outside Harlan's horsepen was more than a shock to his senses. Women didn't visit the Flying H. As far as that went, hardly anyone ever came to see him or his daughter, Emily.

He dropped the yearling's lead rope and slowly walked over to the fence where the woman stood. "Hello," he said.

She extended her hand through the fence to him. "Hello, Mr. Hamilton. I'm Rose Murdock, your neighbor on the Bar M."

Yes, Harlan remembered as his eyes skimmed over the long, chestnut braid lying against her right breast, her fair, faintly freckled skin and clear gray eyes. He'd been visiting Tomas one day and while they'd been looking over some of his racehorse stock, she'd approached the two of them to give her father a telephone message.

She'd barely spoken to Harlan that day, but he hadn't felt slighted by her lukewarm greeting. He'd figured she'd taken him for a wrangler in need of work rather than a friend of her father's. At the time, all three of the Murdock sisters had been single. But he'd read a few weeks ago where one of them had married Sheriff Pardee. An acquaintance of his had once made a joking remark that Harlan might enjoy a redhead cooking his meals and warming his bed. Harlan had ignored the suggestion. He didn't want or need his bed warmed by a redheaded Murdock or any woman for that matter. One wife had been enough for him.

"So Miss Murdock, is this a social call or can I help you with something?"

The words "social call" brought a heated stain to Rose's cheeks. "I don't call on men socially. I'm here to talk to you about something I observed on the ranch awhile ago."

Realizing he was still holding onto her hand, Harlan dropped it and motioned toward a piñon standing a few feet away. "Let's get out of this sun," he suggested, then stepped out of the corral and latched the gate behind him.

Her heart thudding with each step she took, Rose followed him to the flimsy shade. "I'm sorry to interrupt your work like this, Mr. Hamilton, but I—"

"There's no need for you to call me Mr. Hamilton. My name is Harlan."

Yes, she'd known his name was Harlan, but calling him by his first name was getting too personal for Rose's taste. Still, she didn't want to offend this man. He was her neighbor and he could make life hell for her and her sisters if he decided to be difficult.

Clearing her throat, she lifted her eyes to his face. Close up, she was immediately struck by the toughness of his features, his rough, leathery skin and hooded brown eyes. A shadow of unshaven beard darkened his chin and jaws, while sweat trickled from beneath his hatband and tracked down his temples.

"Well, Harlan," she finally managed to say, "what I'm here about is the fence running between our properties. It's been cut, and cattle have been herded from your pasture onto my pasture. Do you know anything about this?"

He remained silent for a long time and Rose eventually felt herself begin to wilt beneath his gaze. She could feel his eyes on her face, her lips, her bosom. Rose had never considered herself attractive to men and to have one look at her as blatantly as this was something she wasn't quite ready to deal with.

"I suppose I should have said something to you or your family before I cut the fence. But I didn't have any idea you'd be riding horseback that far away from your ranch."

Rose stared at him with wide eyes. "I have to ride fence just like you do, Mr. Hamilton. And for you to take it for granted that a certain part of our boundary fence would be ignored is, well—it's insulting."

"I told you to call me Harlan," he said with a sudden flare of his nostrils. "And as for the fence, I might remind you that your father and I were equal partners building it."

Rose hadn't any idea the man had contributed toward the fence. She'd thought the Bar M had shouldered all the labor and expense. Embarrassed by her ignorance, Rose glanced away from him. "I wasn't aware of that. But I was concerned when I found the cut wires. There wasn't any way of my knowing you'd done it."

He grimaced. "Believe me, Miss Murdock, I didn't get any enjoyment in tearing down the fence. But I hardly had any choice in the matter. I'm in bad need of water over here, and before your father died, he gave me permission to use the river on your land."

Surprised by his admission, she said, "Surely the river runs through your property, too."

"Only parts of it. The pasture where I cut the wire has nothing but a pond and it dried up two weeks ago."

"I know it's been dry but—"

"Dry! It's been hell for the past two months! There's plenty of people around here who are hurting for water. We just aren't as blessed as you Murdocks."

Blessed! He didn't know the half of it, Rose thought a little angrily. Their father had died and left them a pile of debts, then they'd discovered that the twin babies abandoned on their front porch were really their half brother and sister. Their father apparently had had an affair with a woman in Las Cruces while their invalid mother had lain dying. And to make matters worse, he'd been sending his mistress an exorbitant amount of money every month. Tomas Murdock's lack of morals and common sense had left Rose, her sisters and aunt in dire straits. No, this man didn't know the half of it!

"We aren't exactly overflowing with water ourselves, Mr.—Harlan. The river is very low."

"At least there's water in it."

"Yes. It's still running," she had to agree.

"Then I think the least you and your sisters can do is share."

Her brows shot upward. "Share?"

He frowned. "I don't know why you find that so incredible. I mean, it's been a year and I haven't seen a cent from you people. I realize Tomas passed on, but that doesn't mean his debts can be ignored."

"Debts?"

In the back of her mind, Rose knew she was beginning to sound like a parrot, but she couldn't help it. This man was tossing remarks at her that she couldn't begin to understand.

Harlan recognized genuine confusion when he saw it. This woman with her smooth, creamy skin and shiny chestnut hair knew nothing of what he was talking about.

"I'm..." he paused as he glanced over his shoulder at the yearling trotting around the dusty corral. "If you'll pardon me a minute, I'll let the yearling loose and we'll go up to the house and talk."

Rose had already been in this man's company far longer than she'd wanted or expected to be.

"Can't you say whatever it is you have to say now? I came over here on horseback, and it's going to take me awhile to get back home as it is."

Surprise lifted his dark brows. "You rode over here?"

"Why, yes," she said. "Is something wrong? Have your

horses been quarantined for sleeping sickness or something?''

He shook his head. "No. There's no problem like that," he assured her but didn't go on to explain that she looked far too fragile and feminine to have ridden several miles in this searing heat. "And you don't have to worry about riding back home," he told her. "I can haul you and your horse to the Bar M."

She unconsciously straightened her shoulders. "That won't be necessary."

"Well, we'll see," he said, then went to tend to the yearling.

Once he was finished, the two of them walked the short distance to the house. At the back, they crossed a ground-level porch, then entered a door which took them directly into a small kitchen.

Dirty dishes were piled in the sink and the remnants of where a meal had been cooked still littered the stove, but the oval Formica table standing in the middle of the room had been cleared and wiped.

Harlan motioned for Rose to take a seat. "We have iced tea or soft drinks if you'd like," he offered.

As Rose pulled out a chair, she immediately started to decline the drink, then suddenly thought better of it. She'd been out in the heat for several hours and had only stopped to drink from her thermos a couple of times. Keeling over with heatstroke was the last thing she wanted to do in front of this man.

"Iced tea would be nice," she told him.

He fixed two glasses of the drink, gave one to Rose, then placed the other one at the end of the table to her left.

"I'll be right back," he said.

Feeling more than awkward, she watched him leave the room. The television was still playing somewhere in another part of the house. Rose supposed Harlan's daughter was watching it and as her gaze wandered around the untidy kitchen, she couldn't help but think the girl was like the yearling he'd been working with earlier. She probably balked at doing anything except what she wanted.

Rose had taken several sips of the cold, sweetened tea when Harlan returned with a folded white paper in his hand.

After taking a seat, he handed her the document. "Before we talk anymore about the water, I think you need to see this."

Rose's heart was suddenly pattering out of control, but whether it was reacting to Harlan's closeness or the dread of what she was about to read, she wasn't sure.

Praying her hands would remain steady, she unfolded the legal-size document and quickly scanned the typewritten paragraphs. By the time she reached the end of the page every last drop of blood had drained from her face. A sick feeling roiled in her stomach.

"This is—unbelievable!" she said in a voice hardly above a whisper.

"Believe me, Miss Murdock, it's legal and binding."

Rose lifted her eyes to his. "I'm not doubting its authenticity," she quickly assured him. "I'm talking about my father—"

Biting down on her lip, she looked away from him. How could Tomas have done such a thing to his family, she wondered sickly. First that woman—his mistress, whom they still hadn't been able to track down! For all they knew she might turn up any day and demand more money, or even worse, her babies back. Now this!

Forcing her gaze back to him, she said, "I must tell you Mr.—Harlan, my sisters and I knew nothing of this. We're, well, actually we're finding that our father kept a good many things from us while he was alive. But this is—I can't imagine what he was thinking!"

Harlan could see she was clearly wounded by the knowledge that her father had borrowed money from him and used the Bar M as collateral. Hell, if his old man had done such a thing to him, he'd be more than wounded, Harlan thought. He'd be wanting to draw blood.

"Did he tell you why he wanted the money?" Rose asked. "Why did he come to you rather than go to the bank?"

The pain in her gray eyes bothered Harlan. He looked away from her as his forefinger unconsciously slid up and down the side of the cold, sweaty glass.

"He didn't say exactly what he wanted the money for and I didn't ask. Tomas was my friend. When I first moved onto this place, he helped me while others didn't bother to offer. Your father didn't have to tell me why he needed the money. I was just glad to be able to help him out. As to why he came to me rather than the bank, well—" Harlan shrugged and forced himself to look at Tomas's daughter. "I got the impression he didn't want to have to do any explaining and that maybe he had already borrowed to the hilt."

It didn't surprise Rose that this man was so intuitive. There was something about his strong presence that told her he'd done, seen and lived a lot in his thirty-some years. He was no man's fool.

Rose's fingers tightened on the promissory note in her hands. "Daddy was—we used his life insurance to pay off his debts. At least, the ones we were aware of. Are you—calling us in on this?"

Harlan glanced at her sharply. She seemed to expect the very worst from him. Was she always so negative? Or was she only reacting that way to him?

"Why, no. I'm not calling you in on the loan."

She felt sick with relief. "That's hard to believe."

Her eyes were full of moisture. She blinked them several times as she looked at the paper in her hands. Harlan suddenly felt like a bastard, although he didn't know why. When he'd loaned Tomas Murdock money, he'd done it to help the older man, not jeopardize his ranch or his family.

"I'm not a loan shark."

With slow, jerky movements, Rose refolded the paper and lay it on the table a few inches from Harlan Hamilton's tough, tanned fingers. "That's obvious. The payment has been overdue for some time now and you haven't notified or billed us. Why?"

Harlan wasn't really sure why. It wasn't as if he was set for money. Since the drought had hit, he could use the thousands he'd lent Tomas. Even in the cooler season of the year, the Flying H needed water wells drilled. But he'd been loathe to collect the debt.

"I knew Tomas had died. And I figured you and your sisters had plenty on your minds as it was."

Rose never had had a high opinion of men, and over the past few months since she'd learned of her daddy's infidelities, she'd lost even more respect for the male gender. To think that this man had considered her and her family's grief before himself was hard for Rose to digest.

"I must tell you...at the present, there's no way we could find the money to pay you back. Even if we sold the last head of cattle we had, we couldn't come up with what our father borrowed from you."

She was telling the truth. Harlan could see that plainly. He could also see that Rose Murdock was not a frivolous woman. She was plainspoken and no-nonsense. What surprised him about her admission was that the Bar M could be that drained of funds.

Harlan had lived here for seven years. His neighbors to the west owned the largest ranch in the county, perhaps one of the largest in the whole state of New Mexico. They raised good cattle and even better horses. They had plenty of rich grazing land along the Hondo river and several skilled cowboys to take care of it all. But what she'd just said about repaying the loan and the fact that she'd been line riding herself told Harlan things had changed drastically on the Bar M.

The whole idea was hard for Harlan to absorb, but not nearly as hard, he figured, as it was for Rose Murdock. "I'm not worried about you paying me back right now."

Nerves clenched her stomach like a vice. "You should be."

"I need water more than I need money."

He took off his battered straw hat and ran a hand through his hair. It was the color of sable and just as shiny. Worn a bit longer than the current fashion, the dark strands fell haphazardly across his forehead and curled around his ears and neck. The front of his shirt was soiled and a large patch of sweat had soaked through the gray material in the middle of his chest. Rose thought he looked a bit like she'd imagined the cowhands did who worked this land when it was still a wild, dangerous territory. Rough, tough and just a little reckless.

"I can't understand you," she said. "You have the power right there—" she pointed at the piece of paper "—to take the Bar M. It could legally be yours now if you wanted to push the issue."

He frowned at her. "I don't want to take your home away from you."

Suddenly it was all too much for Rose. Pressing the heel of her hand against her forehead, she closed her eyes and let out a long, weary sigh.

"I came over here," she said, "to ask you about a simple cut in the fence. Instead, I learn that the Bar M owes you several thousand dollars!" Opening her eyes, she turned her gaze to his face. "You could have at least warned us about this!"

She sounded both accusing and defeated. Harlan wanted

to comfort her somehow but realized there wasn't much he could do. He couldn't tell her to simply forget the loan, that he would dissolve her father's debt. The money had been a big part of Harlan's savings. He'd worked, scrimped and sacrificed for years to obtain that much money. He couldn't afford to give it away, no matter how bad he felt for this woman.

Draining half his tea, he ran his hand through his hair again, then got to his feet and moved to the other side of the room. He'd never had a woman in his kitchen before. His wife had died before he and Emily had moved to New Mexico. The sight of Rose Murdock sitting at the table with her hat hanging against her back, her light red hair curling wildly about her face and her small breasts jutting against her denim shirt was more than a little distracting for him.

"I'm sure this was the last thing you expected or wanted to hear," he said, moving over to the sink filled with dirty dishes. "And I wish like hell your father had never borrowed the money in the first place."

"But he did," Rose said quietly. She looked over at him as he turned on the tap and squirted soap over the mound of plates and glasses. "How soon will you need a payment?"

"It isn't necessary to discuss the money part of it now. I'd rather talk about water."

This man literally had the Bar M in his hands if he wanted it, yet he chose not to move in for the kill. Rose couldn't believe he was being so bighearted. What was he doing, waiting like a hawk for his prey to weaken?

"How can we help you?"

His back turned to Rose, he said, "You can open up part of your land to me."

Chapter Two

Of the three Murdock sisters, Rose had always been the quiet, levelheaded one. She was sweet tempered and rarely ever showed an outward display of emotion. But the shock of Harlan's words shot her to her feet. "Open our land to you?"

Harlan glanced over his shoulder. Her breasts were heaving and her hands were fluttering helplessly at her sides. He could see she was struggling not to be upset, but the flash in her gray eyes and the quaver in her voice told him she was losing the battle to hold on to her emotions.

"Back in east Texas my friends told me I was crazy to move out here on the New Mexico desert. But I've come to love this place and I don't want to lose it, or my cattle." He turned and leveled his dark eyes on her. "I expect you'd rather let me use a pasture with water than meet the stipulations of your daddy's loan."

Something about this rancher made Rose forget to keep her distance. With a boldness that was completely foreign to her nature, she marched over to within a step of him.

"Are you threatening me? Is that what this is all about?"

Suddenly there was a comical twist of frustration on his face. "Look, Rose, if I'd wanted to take your home away from you I could have done it legally several months ago! I'm not a vulture. I'm just a man trying to make a living. All I'm asking for is a little help from the Bar M. And under the circumstances, I don't think that's asking too much."

Of course he had every right to ask for water. In fact, Rose knew she should be down on her knees thanking God that Harlan Hamilton wasn't demanding more. Still, the idea of opening the ranch to someone else was like inviting a stranger into her bedroom. The Bar M had been Murdock land for more than forty years. No one had so much as leased a foot of it, or even walked across it. Each section of pasture was like a room in the ranch house. She didn't want interlopers in her home.

With a surrendering shake of her head, Rose said, "No, you're not asking too much. But I must tell you I'm in the same situation you are, Harlan. What bit of grass I have left is burning and I need it for my own cattle."

Harlan wasn't a man to take advantage of anyone who happened to be down on their luck, and that included a beautiful woman. But at the moment he was having tough luck of his own.

"I can understand that. But I need water wells drilled and pumps installed. Doing that takes lots of money. Money that I loaned to Tomas," Harlan replied. "I have no intention of going into debt, and I'm not going to sell my cattle. If it makes you feel any better, you can count the use of your water as the first payment on the loan."

Rose was backed into a corner with no way out. She had no choice but to let him have what he asked for and hope and pray his wants would stop there.

Squaring her shoulders, she jammed her hat back on her

head, then tugged the brim down on her forehead. "I'm not a difficult woman, Harlan, nor am I foolish. I'll meet you tomorrow at the boundary fence and we'll decide what to do with your cattle and mine. Now I should be heading home before dark catches me."

She turned to go. Harlan immediately called her back.

"If you galloped all the way back to the Bar M you couldn't beat the dark. I'll take you."

"My horse—"

"The stock trailer is already hooked onto the truck. It won't be any problem to take you both home."

If it wasn't for Pie stepping on a sidewinder in the dark, she would have insisted on riding back alone. She didn't want to climb into a vehicle with this man. In fact, if she didn't get away from him soon, she was certain she'd never be able to breathe properly again.

"Very well," she conceded.

Harlan walked over to an open doorway leading to other parts of the house. "Emily?"

A few moments passed before the teenager appeared in the doorway. "You wanted me?" she asked her father.

Harlan introduced his daughter to Rose, then added, "I'm going to drive Miss Murdock back home. Would you like to come with us?"

The girl threw a suspicious glance at Rose. "No."

Harlan sighed. "You haven't been off the place for several days. It would do you good to get out of the house, Emily."

Having been a schoolteacher the past five years had taught Rose many things about children. She knew that underneath petulance was usually a need for attention or love. As for Emily, there was a sad, depressed look about the girl that tugged at Rose's heart.

"I know what the Murdock place looks like," Emily said with a toss of her head.

"If that's the way you feel about it," Harlan said to her, "then I expect you to have this kitchen clean by the time I get back."

The bored look on the girl's face suddenly turned indignant. "But, Daddy," she protested. "I'll miss my program and—"

"No buts. You didn't want to go, so stay here and make yourself useful. And turn that darn TV off. If I come back and hear it on, it's going to stay off for a week."

Turning to Rose, he nodded toward the door leading to the back porch. "If you're ready, let's go."

Rose looked at the teenage girl. "Goodbye, Emily. I hope we meet again, soon."

For a moment, Rose thought Harlan's daughter was going to rebuff her but then a faint smile crossed the girl's thin face.

"Goodbye, Rose."

Once the two of them were outside the house, Harlan said, "I hope you'll overlook Emily's rudeness. She's been in one of her moods lately."

"I used to be a schoolteacher, so I'm accustomed to teenagers' moods," Rose replied.

They rounded the house and Rose was relieved to see that Pie was only a few steps away from where she'd left him. She reached for the horse's reins, but Harlan immediately took them from her. As he led the horse toward the barn Rose followed him. The sun was already down and shadows were lengthening on the dry, cracked ground beneath their feet. While they walked, Rose kept her eyes on the dusty toes of her boots.

"You say you were a teacher. Does that mean you'll not be teaching when school begins in September?"

"The ranch needs me now," she said frankly.

Harlan glanced over at her downcast head. Things were

obviously much worse at the Bar M than he'd expected and that worried him for more reasons than one.

A few minutes later they were traveling west across Flying H land. The evening air was beginning to cool. Rose removed her hat so that the breeze coming through the open cab would blow her hair.

As the ranch house disappeared behind them, Rose couldn't help but wonder if Harlan's daughter was cleaning the kitchen or watching TV. Did her daddy spoil her, misunderstand her, love her? The questions pestered her until she finally said, "It must be a very quiet life for Emily during the summer months. Does she do any activities with friends her age?"

"Sometimes. But it's not exactly easy for me to drive her into Ruidoso for entertainment."

"I understand. We live a long way from town, too, you know."

She was hugging the door. Her hands were folded primly on her lap, her eyes fixed straight ahead. Each time Harlan glanced her way she remained as stiff as when they'd first left the house.

"I don't think Emily's problem is all boredom. The way you saw her is pretty much how she's been for the past year. At first I thought it was her age. But now I'm not so sure."

Rose never encouraged conversation with single men. She found it usually led to awkward situations. Especially when the man insisted on getting personal. But she couldn't remain indifferent to Harlan. With his long, lean body sitting only inches away, his earthy, masculine scent swirling around her, she was more aware of him than she could ever remember being of any man.

"How long has your daughter been without her mother?"

A grimace marred his face. "You know she doesn't have a mother?"

Rose nodded, then quickly explained, "When I came to your house I asked Emily if I could speak with you or her mother. She told me she didn't have a mother."

"She can be blunt at times." Harlan downshifted the truck and stopped as the dirt road they'd been traveling intersected with the main highway. Glancing at her, he added, "Karen died when Emily was going on seven years old. She's thirteen now."

Pulling onto the oozy asphalt, Harlan headed west toward the foot of the mountains and the Bar M ranch.

Three miles passed before Rose could think of a reply. She said, "That's a long time for a child to be without a mother."

Harlan let out a snort. "I damn well didn't choose it that way."

The sharpness of his voice swung Rose's gaze around to him. His profile was hard and unmoving, making it obvious to her that he was still bitter over losing his wife.

But that wasn't her problem, Rose quickly reminded herself. Nor was his sullen daughter. The Bar M was drowning in debt, and if he had a mind to, this man sitting next to her could push her the rest of the way under.

Dear God, how was she going to tell her sisters, Chloe and Justine, and her Aunt Kitty that Tomas had borrowed several thousand dollars and put the ranch up as collateral? Just thinking about it left her numb with fear.

"I'm sure you didn't choose to lose your wife," Rose said quietly.

Harlan rubbed a hand over his face. "I thought you meant—" He turned his head and his eyes searched her face. "Some people think I'm being cruel to Emily by not marrying again. I figured you were thinking the same thing. Were you?"

Rose couldn't believe they were having this discussion. She didn't even know this man. She didn't want to know him. But each passing minute seemed to be showing her another slice of his personality.

A faint frown drew her dark auburn brows together. "I wouldn't be so presumptuous as to advise you about your family life, Mr.—Harlan."

A quirk of humor moved his lips. "I wasn't asking for your advice. I was asking what you thought."

"Why?"

"I beg your pardon?" he asked.

He'd mentioned east Texas and from the sound of his drawl, Rose figured he must have grown up in that part of the country. She couldn't deny the soft lilt of his voice did pleasant things to her senses.

"Why do you want to know what I think? You don't even know me."

Shrugging, he fixed his eyes on the darkening highway. "It's been a long time since I've talked to a woman and since Emily is a girl, well, I sometimes wonder if I can see things the way you females do."

"Have you met a woman you'd like to marry?"

He cast her a dry glance, then suddenly burst out with a short laugh. "Rose, there isn't a woman on earth I'd want to marry."

His mocking attitude stiffened her spine to a rigid line of indignation. There wasn't a man on earth she'd want to marry either, but she didn't go around telling any of them such a thing. She didn't like men, but that hardly made her want to insult them.

"Then I think it best you stay single and—forget about what your friends say."

The little grin he gave her said she'd spoken the very words he'd wanted to hear. "You know, Rose, I think you're gonna be my kind of woman."

* * *

Ten minutes later, Rose was back home on the Bar M unsaddling Pie in the dimly lit stables. As she jerked on the worn latigo, Harlan's words continued to gnaw at her craw.

His kind of woman.

She'd wanted to reach across the seat and slap his face. She, who had trouble bringing her boot down on a scorpion, wanted to commit an act of physical violence against another human being! What had come over her?

With a tired grunt, she swung the saddle over the top rail of the empty stall, then slapped the bridle across the seat.

"Rose?"

At the sound of the female voice, Rose turned to see Chloe standing a few steps behind her. Like her sisters, she was a redhead—although her straight, shoulder length hair was a much deeper auburn than that of her siblings. And unlike Rose and Justine, Chloe was petite. But her temper and strength made up for her small stature. At the moment she was frowning with concern.

"Is something wrong?"

Rose forced herself to breathe deeply. The last thing she wanted was for Chloe to think a man had gotten under her sister's skin.

"I'm just hot and tired."

Chloe moved closer, her eyes wandering keenly over Rose's flushed face. "You're hot and tired when you come in every evening, but you don't always look like you've been tangling with a bull."

A bull? Well, Harlan certainly had a few similarities to one, she couldn't help thinking.

"Are you finished here?" Rose glanced down the long line of compartments to see if all the horses were back in their stalls. "We need to go up to the house and talk."

"Talk? What's happened now?"

A year ago, Chloe would never have responded with

such a negative question. Their father had still been alive then, the ranch, or so it had appeared to her and her sisters, had been thriving and rain had continued to keep the grass growing right up until frost.

But this summer nothing had seemed to go right and Rose supposed Chloe's usually bright outlook had finally started crumbling under the problems they'd been forced to face. As for herself, Rose was very nearly too numb to feel anything except a staggering weight on her shoulders.

"Let's go find Aunt Kitty," Rose said while nudging Chloe toward the open doorway of the stable. "I only want to have to tell this story once."

Back at the house, the sisters entered an overly warm kitchen to find Kitty, a petite woman in her sixties with short gray hair. She was setting the table and didn't stop to look at her nieces. "It's almost ready, girls. Go wash and get the twins from the playpen. Their baby food is heating."

Minutes later, gathered around the dining table, Chloe took on the job of feeding Anna, while Rose assumed the task of feeding Adam. The twins were eight months old and starting to cut teeth. For the past week both babies had been fussy with sore gums. But tonight they appeared to be in better humor. Rose was relieved. She adored her little brother and sister and couldn't bear to see them in any sort of pain.

"Okay Rose, tell us what happened today," Chloe said as she offered a spoon of pureed green beans to Anna. "You found another dead cow while you were riding fence?"

"For heaven's sake, what now?" Kitty asked wearily.

Rose decided it would do no good to delay the telling. "The fence between us and the Flying H has been cut and cattle herded onto our land."

"What?" Chloe practically yelled the question.

Totally bewildered, Kitty asked, "Who would have done such a thing?"

"I rode over to the Flying H and confronted Harlan Hamilton about it," Rose told them. "He admitted that he'd done it."

Chloe's mouth fell open. Kitty simply stared at her niece. When neither of them said anything, Rose made an impatient gesture with her hand. "Don't look at me like that."

"Like what?" Kitty asked with a puzzled frown.

"Like you're wondering what gave the timid spinster enough courage to go see a man," she said with disgust.

"Rose! None of us think of you as a timid spinster," Chloe countered. "That's your own way of thinking."

Frustrated because she still couldn't gather her nerves together, Rose closed her eyes and drew in a deep breath. "I'm sorry," she told the two women, "I'm still feeling sorta testy."

Kitty and Chloe exchanged worried glances. Rose never felt testy over anything—quietly concerned maybe, but never angry or irritated.

"Why? What happened between you and our neighbor?" Chloe asked.

"Like I said, I went to see him. I didn't want to, but I made myself." Rose offered Adam a spoonful of pureed chicken. The baby smacked his lips in appreciation. "And I guess it's a good thing I did, or we might have—"

"What?" Kitty prompted when Rose stopped in midsentence.

"You're not going to believe what he showed me."

"His naked chest?" Chloe asked dryly.

Rose shot her sister a cool look of disapproval. "The man is running out of water."

"So are a lot of other people around here," Kitty spoke up. "Why, Vida was just telling me yesterday they were having to haul their drinking water from Ruidoso."

"So is that why Mr. Hamilton cut our fence and drove his cattle onto our land? To give them a drink?" Chloe asked in disbelief. "I can't really see what good that was going to do. Cattle have to have water every day. Or—" She looked at her sister with raised eyebrows. "He didn't leave them on our land, did he?"

Rose shook her head. "No, he didn't leave them on our land, but he intends for us to—" She couldn't go on. Her throat closed around the words, forcing her to swallow several times before she could speak. "He wants us to open up the Bar M to him so that his cattle can reach our part of the river."

The two women stared at Rose in stunned silence, then finally Chloe burst out laughing.

"You know, I always wondered why that man was single," she said once her laughter had trailed away to a chuckle. "He's got looks to die for, but apparently he doesn't have a brain to go with them."

"Just hush, Chloe, you haven't heard it all," Rose scolded wearily.

"You mean there's more?"

Adam was banging his fist on the high-chair tray. Rose quickly pushed another spoonful of food at the baby.

"Oh, yes. It seems that several months ago, more than a year to be exact, our father borrowed money from Harlan Hamilton."

"No!" Kitty said with a sharp gasp.

The humor suddenly vanished from Chloe's face. "How much?"

Rose repeated the amount and once again the two women stared blankly at her.

"The worst part is," Rose continued, "Daddy put the Bar M up as collateral."

Chloe rocketed to her feet. "He couldn't have! He wouldn't have!"

Her face stiff, Rose said, "He did. Harlan has it on document. And I'll assure you it was all very legal."

"You mean, if we don't or can't repay Mr. Hamilton, the ranch could belong to him?" Kitty asked fearfully.

Rose nodded. "That's just about the size of it."

"So what are we going to do?" Chloe asked sinkingly. "If we sell our stock there's no way the ranch can make money!"

Adam began pushing away the offered spoon, indicating to Rose he was full. She wiped the baby's face and hands, then began filling her own plate. She wasn't going to let what her father had done, or what Harlan might do, ruin her supper.

"We're going to open up our land to Mr. Hamilton and hope that he'll be patient about the loan. Right now, he says water is the only thing he wants from us," Rose told the two women.

Like a fallen rock Chloe dropped back into her chair. "Oh Rose, you're so gullible where men are concerned. You haven't been around them enough to know they'll tell you anything that suits them—no matter how far from the truth it is."

Rose leveled a dark look at her sister. "Oh, I think you know I learned all about men a long time ago, Chloe. That's exactly why I stay away from them. But as for Harlan— we have no choice but to trust him. He's holding all the cards."

Chloe sagged against the back of her chair.

Kitty looked at Rose. "What do you think about this Mr. Hamilton, Rose? Do you think he can be trusted?"

Did she? Since her ordeal with Peter more than eight years ago, Rose had never trusted any man, except her father. And even that had turned out to be a mistake. She'd be a fool to believe Harlan was sincere. Yet for some reason she wanted to think he was different from the rest, that maybe he was one of those few men like her sister's husband, Roy Pardee. An honest man with morals and a good heart.

"I don't know, Aunt Kitty. I found out he's a widower with a teenage daughter. He appears to be a responsible man and father, but who's to say? We thought Daddy was a responsible man and father."

"Tomas must have been a very troubled man to do what he did. Having an affair with that woman, paying her all that money and now this! I just thank God my sister Lola isn't alive to know about it." Kitty shook her head sadly. "So what's going to happen next?"

Rose took a long drink of ice water. She'd never felt so exhausted in her life and to think of getting up and facing Harlan in the morning was nearly more than she could bear.

"First thing tomorrow I'm going to meet Harlan at the cut in the fence and we're going to decide what to do about the cattle. As for the money, I'm sure you both know we don't have it and there's no chance we will have it for a long time to come. He says his use of our water will count for a payment on the loan. I don't know how much money that means, but I'll find out."

The kitchen went quiet, except for the babies, who were squealing and straining to grab the other's face across their high-chair trays.

Rose finished the food on her plate, then lifted Adam into her arms. The baby nuzzled his head against her neck and she savored his innocent affection. The twins were the only good thing to come out of this mess their father had made. And whether the law ever managed to track down their mother or not, the whole family was determined to keep them and raise them as true Murdocks. "I'm going to give Adam a bath and get ready for bed. Will one of you call Justine and tell her the news?"

Kitty nodded solemnly. "I will. Maybe Roy might have some idea that could help us."

"Roy's a good sheriff, but I don't think he can help us out of this mess," Rose said, then turned to leave the kitchen.

"Rose," Chloe called after her.

Rose turned to look at her younger sister. "Would you rather I met Mr. Hamilton in the morning?"

She and Chloe had always been opposites. Chloe was normally bubbly and outspoken and very self-confident, whereas Rose was just quiet, old Rose. Yet there had always been a deep love between them and Rose could feel it now more than ever.

"Thanks for offering, Chloe, but this is—well, it's something I have to do myself. After Daddy died we agreed that the horses were your responsibility and the cattle mine. I'm not going to run from my job just because I don't like dealing with a man."

"We never said we couldn't help each other out, if the other needed it," Chloe said gently.

A wan smile touched Rose's face. "I know. But oddly enough Harlan Hamilton doesn't scare me. It's just that—there's something about the man that bothers me." Adam tugged on a loose tendril of her hair. Rose absently kissed the baby's cheek. "But I can put up with him for as long as it takes to get this ranch back to a solid business again. And I'm making a promise right now. Harlan Hamilton is never going to own the Bar M."

Chapter Three

Long before Rose reached the faint bend in the river, Harlan spotted her on the sorrel. From the hill where he sat on his black mare he watched and waited for her to ride closer.

She was dressed as she had been yesterday in a pair of worn jeans, brown boots and a gray felt hat. The only difference was her shirt. This one was deep green and buttoned tightly at the cuffs and throat.

Last night after he'd taken the woman home, he'd found it nearly impossible to stop thinking about her and he couldn't figure why. True, she had a quiet, natural beauty. But he'd seen plenty of good-looking women since Karen had died and none of them had stirred him in any way. Yet there was something about Rose Murdock that made him itch in all the wrong places.

Nudging the mare's sides, he decided to ride down the slope to meet her and the spotted blue dog trotting at her heels.

"Good morning," she said as he stopped abreast of her.

"Good morning," he drawled.

She shifted in the saddle as his dark brown eyes scanned her face. She didn't know why the man had to look at her like he enjoyed it. She was too thin to have much of a figure and her features were sharp and angular. The only nice things about her were full lips and gray luminous eyes. But in Rose's opinion nothing about her warranted a second glance.

"I've talked with my family about letting you use some of the ranch," she said to him.

"And?"

And? Did he honestly think they were in a position to refuse him? Rose wondered. She said, "Of course they're in agreement. They're leaving it up to me and you to decide which parts of the land would work best for all of us."

"I'm glad they understand my problem."

Rose came close to groaning out loud. His problem? All he needed was a little water. She and her sisters needed a miracle.

"My sisters and I would like to know how much money you're willing to allow us for our water," she told him.

He studied her for a moment, then named an amount that Rose considered surprisingly generous.

"I think that's more than fair," she said awkwardly as her eyes skittered away from his tough face.

Looks to die for. That's the way Chloe had described him. Rose didn't know about that, but she knew whenever she looked at him she couldn't think or breathe or do anything but gawk like a naive teenager. Her reaction to him was downright silly. But she didn't know how to stop it.

Harlan motioned toward the section of land they were presently on. "I have a hundred head to graze and water. Can this spot do that? It's the closest one to me and the most feasible one to use. Or do you have cattle in here now?"

She nodded. "Fifty head. But I can move them."

"That's a lot of trouble."

It was. But she was getting pretty used to dealing with trouble. First they found babies abandoned on the doorstep, then they discovered their father had been blackmailed by the mother into making exorbitant payments, and now this loan to Harlan Hamilton. Rose couldn't imagine what else might turn up as a result of their father's reckless behavior.

"There's no other choice," Rose told him.

"Where is your open pasture?" he asked.

Her eyes flickered back to Harlan. The gold of the morning sun was rising behind him, outlining his thick shoulders, the rolled brim of his black hat and the dark curls lying against his neck. He looked like a moonlighter, something the old men of the west called a cattle thief. Could she trust him with her cattle? Her land? Herself?

"Several miles from here."

Rubbing his unshaved jaws, he thoughtfully studied the land spread to the west of them. The river was dry in spots, but in other places the water was deep and cool. If heaven had a name, the Bar M had to be it, he thought.

"I see you didn't bring a wrangler with you," he said to Rose.

Her eyes on Pie's tangled mane, she said, "I don't have a wrangler. I'm it."

Harlan couldn't have been more stunned if Queen, his mare, had suddenly started bucking sky-high. This woman was taking care of several thousand acres of land and cattle on her own? No. He couldn't believe it.

"I'm not saying this because I think you're incompetent, but I just don't believe..." He broke off with a shake of his head. "Surely you have help of some kind."

She combed her fingers through Pie's long mane, then patted his neck. The horse was her help, her companion, her very best buddy. These days she spent more time with him than she did anyone.

"Pie here is my help. And Amos my heeler," she motioned toward the dog, waiting quietly at her horse's hocks. "Believe me, he's a lot better than a handful of lazy wranglers."

He looked skeptically at her, the sorrel and the scroungy dog. "I'm sure he's a good horse and the dog is no doubt trained to work cattle, but—"

"You don't have a hired hand, do you?" she interrupted.

"Well, no, but my ranch is half the size of yours."

She lifted her chin proudly. Not for anything would she let him know how exhausted she was by the end of the day, how weary she was when she rose before dawn to start all over again. Some days she didn't know if she could take another step. But the idea of losing her home drove her on.

"It takes a little more effort. We have someone to cut and bale our alfalfa for us and of course we have to have a farrier over pretty often to shoe Chloe's horses, but other than that we pretty much do things for ourselves."

What would Tomas think if he knew how hard his daughters were working? Harlan wondered. And what had happened to get the place in such shape? Tomas himself? Or had his daughters high-rolled all their money away?

"I know last night you implied things were tight. I didn't realize you meant—well, I hadn't heard you'd let all your hired help go."

If that was the case, then he probably hadn't heard about the twins, or her father's sordid affair that had produced them. Rose couldn't help but wonder what Harlan would think of his old friend when he did finally hear the story.

Rose glanced pointedly at the watch strapped to her wrist. "Well, if you're ready, I think we'd better see if we can find my cattle and get them out of here. This might take awhile."

"Not yet."

Rose cut him a glance. "Why? What are you waiting for?"

"Emily is coming to help. In fact, she should be here any time now." He reined Queen up the slope. "I'll go see if I can spot her."

Rose followed close behind him. "Emily knows about riding and herding cattle?"

He shot her a dry look over his shoulder. "Emily was born on a ranch back in east Texas and she's lived on the Flying H for seven years. Like you, she knows what it's all about."

"You taught her?"

"It's just me and her. I may come up short at being a stand-in mother, but as her daddy, I've taught her all the things I could. That may not seem like much to you, Rose, but..." he paused and shrugged, "someday it might help her."

The two of them rode on to the top of the slope, then pulled their mounts to a stop. As they waited for Emily to appear, Rose considered what Harlan had just told her.

Teaching Emily about ranching was as much or more than what Tomas had taught her. She'd hate to imagine what sort of shape she and her sisters would be in now if they'd been raised as helpless females. Still, she couldn't imagine not having a mother's soft hand to wipe away a tear, brush her hair, help her pick out a dress for the junior high prom.

Rose had been devastated when she'd lost her own mother a little over a year ago. But at least she'd had her love and guidance while she'd been growing up. Emily had been robbed at a very vulnerable time in her life. Did Harlan realize that?

Only a minute or two passed before Emily came riding up on a big Appaloosa. Like Rose, she was dressed for riding in the sun and the brush. A smile on her face, she appeared to be much perkier this morning than she'd been last night.

"Good morning, Rose. I hope you don't mind me tagging along. Daddy thought I might be a help."

Rose smiled at the girl. "I'm very grateful that you're going to help. Since I don't have any wranglers anymore, it'll just be us three and Amos."

The teenager stared at Rose in pretty much the same way her father had. "You don't have help on your ranch?"

"Not right now," Rose told her. "We've had to do a little cutting back."

Harlan wondered what it cost Rose to admit to having financial problems. The woman obviously had pride and he respected her for that. He also respected the fact that she hadn't given up. She was working hard to keep her home together. If she had caused some of the money problems on the Bar M, she was certainly trying to make up for it now.

Wanting to lighten the moment he grinned at both women. "Too bad, honey," he teased Emily. "There won't be any young cowboys for you to show off for."

Emily groaned and tossed her head. "Oh, Daddy, you know I don't like boys."

"Not yet, huh?" he said, then gave Rose a conspiratorial wink.

Rose couldn't remember the last time a man had winked at her. Feeling her cheeks turning pink, she quickly reined Pie away from him. "We'd better get moving," she said matter-of-factly.

Fortunately the Bar M cattle were feeding on a patch of prickly pear not far from the pasture Rose intended to move them into. With Amos barking and circling the herd, it wasn't too difficult for the three of them to bunch the cattle in a tight wad.

Because of the heat, they moved the animals at a slow walk. Even so, fine dust boiled high in the air and covered the three of them. Rose pulled a handkerchief from her jeans pocket and rode over to Emily, who was coughing and waving her hand in front of her face.

"Do you want my handkerchief?" Rose asked her.

Her face brown from the flying dirt, Emily grinned with appreciation, but shook her head. "Thank you, Rose. But you should keep it for yourself. I'll be all right."

It was difficult for Rose to believe this was the same girl who had been whining about washing a sinkful of dishes. So far Emily hadn't complained about anything. In fact, she was working just as hard as Rose to get the job done.

"Then why don't you ride up toward the front of the herd?" Rose suggested to her. "It won't be as dusty up there. Your father and I can watch things back here."

Emily nodded and urged the Appaloosa forward. "Thanks, Rose!"

Rose tied the handkerchief over her nose and mouth, then swung in place a few yards away from Harlan at the back of the herd. She was surprised to see he was watching her.

What was he thinking, she wondered. That all of this would someday be his? Well, thinking was as close as he was ever going to get, she silently promised. She'd sell every last cow and calf on the place and beg every bank in the state before she'd lose this ranch to him, or any man.

"How much farther?" he called over to her.

She wiped her forehead with the back of her forearm. "About a quarter of a mile. We're almost there."

He nodded and she noticed that unlike her and Emily, he appeared to be coping with the dust as though it wasn't any more irritating than a pesky fly.

"I sent Emily up toward the front to get her out of the dust," she told him.

"I noticed."

He didn't say more. Rose didn't expect him to, but something about the expression on his face made her gaze linger longer than it should have. Suddenly his eyes softened and she felt at that moment it was just him and her against the world.

As if he'd read her thoughts, he said, "We're going to get through this, Rose. The both of us."

Maybe they would, she thought. But what would it be like once the rain eventually came, the debt was finally paid and the two of them went back to simply being neighbors again? She'd probably never see him after that.

The thought should have comforted her, even given her something to look forward to. But strangely enough she felt bothered by the idea. Although she couldn't understand why. Harlan wasn't her type. No man was her type. She'd do well to remember that.

By the time the three of them left Rose's cattle safely secured on fresh pasture, it was noon. Harlan suggested they eat lunch before starting the task of moving his cattle onto Bar M land.

Down by the river, Rose found a smooth spot beneath a poplar and pulled out the lunch she'd packed in her saddlebags.

As she spread the containers of food on the ground in front of her, Harlan walked up behind her. "You know, you never cease to amaze me."

The sound of his voice jerked her head up and around. She'd thought he was still tending the horses, not looming over her shoulder. The sight of him standing so close set her heart pounding heavily.

"Why do you say that?" she asked, trying her best to sound casual.

A faint smile tugged at his mouth as he looked down at her dusty face. She wasn't comfortable in his company.

He'd known that the moment he'd walked up to her yesterday evening and she'd introduced herself. Her voice had been cool, yet her glances had been shy. Now the more Harlan was around her, the more he wondered why she wasn't married. She must still be in her early twenties, and when she looked at him with her clear gray eyes, he got the impression that she was far more innocent than her years.

"I never expected you to have your lunch with you."

Frowning, she turned her attention to the sandwich in her hand. "I take food out with me every day. I never know when I'll be too far away from the ranch house to make it back for lunch. Besides, it's always wise to at least carry a thermos of water or some sort of drink with you in this country."

"That's what I'm talking about," he said. He sank to the ground a few feet away from her and leaned his back against a half-dead cottonwood. "Most women wouldn't be so prepared. Hell, most women would be lost out here like this. But you seem right at home in the saddle, herding cows."

She bit into a ham sandwich and told herself not to look at him. She didn't like it when her senses went haywire. And that's what the sight of him did to her, she realized. It crippled her brain. "I was born on this ranch, Harlan. I am home, here."

He drew up one knee and rested his forearm across it. As he watched Emily splash in the river with Amos, he thought about the home he'd left in east Texas, the wife he'd buried there and the home he'd tried to build here.

The Flying H had most everything they needed. A fairly nice house and several barns. Cattle and horses to work the place, cats and dogs for pets, two vehicles to get where they needed to go and a regular pew at church on Sunday.

It was a seemingly normal household. Yet the place had

never felt exactly like home to Harlan. And now he knew why. It was missing a woman. Others had pointed the problem out to him before, but he'd blindly refused to see it. He hadn't wanted to see anything except the memories of his wife. The way it had been with her and the way he'd wished it could have been now.

But Rose had opened his eyes. How or why, Harlan couldn't figure. Nor did he know what, if anything, he was going to do about it.

"You like ranching, or would you prefer to be teaching in a classroom?" Harlan asked as he pulled a sandwich from his own saddlebag.

"I like being needed," she answered, then glanced over to his face. His expression told her he didn't quite understand.

She gestured with her hand to the land around them. "Before Daddy passed away, he had men to take care of all this. There was no need for me to ride fence, spread feed and hay, doctor sick cows, or search for newborn calves. But that's all changed."

The cellophane out of the way, he bit into the sandwich. After he'd swallowed, he asked, "You didn't feel needed when you were teaching?"

She thought about his question. "Oh, yes. I did. But there're always other teachers to take your place. There's no one who can take my place here on the ranch," she told him, then with a little mocking laugh added, "at least, no one who'd work for my salary."

Emily waded out of the shallow river and joined them in the dappled shade of the trees. Amos followed and before Rose could shoo him away, he shook, spraying water over the three of them.

"I guess he thought we all needed a shower," Harlan said with wry humor.

Rose wiped at the drops sliding down her chin, then

pointed sternly at the dog. "Amos, get over there in the shade and behave or you won't get the sandwich I brought for you."

Amos whined in protest, but did exactly what his mistress told him. Emily was more than impressed by the dog's behavior.

"Gosh, none of our dogs are that obedient. If you tell them to do something, they just ignore you."

Harlan chuckled. "Sorta like you do me."

Emily groaned. "Oh Daddy, you're going to have Rose thinking I'm spoiled. And you know I'm not."

"Rose can probably figure that out for herself," Harlan told his daughter. "She used to be a schoolteacher."

Emily dug into her father's saddlebag for a sandwich. "Why aren't you a teacher now? You don't like kids or something?"

Brushing the crumbs from her fingers, Rose reached for her thermos of lemonade. "I like kids and teaching. But I need to work at home now."

"A few months ago, Rose's father died of a heart attack," Harlan gently explained to Emily. "That's why she and her sisters are...having a rough time of it right now."

An achy lump suddenly collected in Rose's throat. He sounded as if he cared, and that touched her in a way she hadn't expected it to. Yet she knew she couldn't afford to get any soft notions about Harlan. Where men were concerned, she always had to be on guard, always be cautious.

Emily looked at Rose with such a sorrowful expression that Rose wanted to take the girl in her arms and hug her tightly.

"Gosh, that's awful. I know, 'cause my mother died when I was little. Do you have a mother?"

Rose shook her head and tried to smile. The last thing she wanted to do was appear maudlin or bitter in front of this girl. Emily needed to know that her young life wasn't ruined because she'd lost her mother. "No. My mother died last year after a long illness."

Emily's eyes widened with sudden dawning. "Daddy, did you hear? Rose...she's like me. She doesn't have a mother."

Harlan nodded at his daughter. "She doesn't have any parents. You still have me, so that makes you a little bit luckier, don't you think?"

A dejected expression settled over the girl's thin features. "I guess," she mumbled. "But all my friends have moms. It doesn't seem fair that I don't."

"I'm your friend and I don't," Rose said gently.

Emily looked across at her and slowly the sadness disappeared from her face. "I guess that makes us kindred spirits. Is that the right word for it? When two people sorta know how the other one feels?"

Rose smiled gently at the girl. "Yes, I think you could safely call us kindred spirits."

A half hour later, after all the food was eaten, the three of them mounted their horses and crossed through the downed fence onto Flying H land. Riding a few paces behind, Harlan watched his daughter continue to chatter with Rose.

He'd never seen her open up to anyone like this before. Not even him. As far as he could remember, today was the first time she'd ever brought up the fact of not having a mother. Before now, she'd always acted as though she'd never had a mother, nor did she ever want one.

His daughter had surprised him today. But then so had Rose. Just looking at her made him feel things he hadn't felt in years, think things that he'd long ago forgotten. She was going to be trouble for him, he realized. Not because she owed him money. But simply because he was going to want her. Maybe he already did.

The deeper the three of them rode into the Flying H, the more open and arid the land became. The hills grew bald. What little grass that hadn't yet burned was hidden beneath a thick covering of sagebrush. Because the grazing was so limited, Harlan's cattle were scattered from here to yonder. It took all afternoon to gather the cattle, then drive them onto Bar M land.

Dusk had fallen when the last calf scampered through the downed fence. Harlan watched the little Hereford catch up with its mother, then stepped down from his mare.

Pulling a pair of pliers from his pocket, he said, "I'm going to wire the fence back together for right now. And in a few days I'll put up a metal gate." He glanced up at Rose, who was still mounted on her horse a few feet away from him. "If you don't mind, that is."

A gate. He'd be connected to her land. She'd be connected to his. It was almost like a marriage between them and that was far too intimate a thought for Rose's peace of mind.

"If you want to put up a gate, it's all right by me. But before you tie those wires back together, you'd better let me ride through so I can head back home."

Turning his back to her, he jerked on the tangled barbed wire. "You just stay where you are. I'm not about to let you ride all the way back home."

Rose wasn't used to a man giving her orders. Even her father had always asked and never told her what to do. Pushing off her hat, she wiped at the grit on her face. Her shoulders were drooping and her legs aching from long hours in the saddle. Pie's coat was caked with dust and stiff with dried, salty sweat. Amos had already flopped down in the shade a few yards away. The dog's feet were sore and his sides were heaving with exhaustion. It would be better for her and her animals to hitch a ride home with him. Still, she hesitated. "Harlan, you took me home last night. I don't expect you to do it again."

Harlan hadn't expected her to do a man's work today, either. But she had. And Harlan knew he would never forget that she'd done it for him. True, she owed him money and didn't have much choice in offering him the land and water. But she could have left him and Emily to deal with their own cattle.

"You're too tired to ride home," Emily spoke as she reined the Appaloosa alongside Rose. "Besides, we'd like for you to stay and eat supper with us. Wouldn't we, Daddy?"

Supper? Harlan never really cooked much, and Emily didn't know how. He couldn't remember a time they'd had someone stay to share a meal. What was his daughter thinking?

He glanced over his shoulder at Rose. "Sure, we'd like for you to stay," he said with feigned casualness. "If you can stand to eat microwave food."

"We have a pizza in the freezer," Emily reminded him. "Will you stay and eat, Rose?"

Rose glanced over at the girl. She'd worked tirelessly today. And now she was looking at Rose with such a hopeful, eager expression that she couldn't bring herself to say no.

"I guess I could stay. If it wouldn't be putting you to any trouble," she said, then glanced at Harlan. He'd already turned his attention back to twisting the barbed wire together. She wished she knew how he really felt about his daughter's invitation. But it wasn't as if she was a girlfriend coming over for a dinner date, she assured herself. She'd simply be a dirty cowhand eating a slice of pizza with her neighbors.

"Oh, it won't be any trouble at all. It's going to be great," Emily said with a happy grin.

As the three of them rode over the sage-covered hills toward the Flying H, Rose's gaze kept drifting over to Harlan. His shirt was wet with sweat and covered with so much dust that it appeared more brown than blue. His legs were long in the stirrups and he sat in the saddle with the ease of a natural horseman.

If Rose had learned anything today, it was that Harlan was as dedicated to his ranch as Rose was to the Bar M. She respected him for that and she was beginning to think he could be trusted up to a point. But he had the power to take her home away from her. She could never lose sight of that fact.

Once they reached the barnyard on the Flying H, Emily tossed her reins to Harlan. "Will you take care of my horse, Daddy? I'm going to run ahead to the house and get things started in the kitchen." She giggled sheepishly as she slid from the saddle. "It might need a little tidying up before Rose sees it."

"I would almost bet it needs a little more than tidying up," Harlan said dryly and motioned her on. "Go ahead. We'll be up to the house in a few minutes."

Rose watched the girl dash off toward the house. Harlan shook his head. "She's excited about having you here," he said. "I guess you can tell."

"I'm very flattered that she seems to like me," Rose admitted.

He dismounted and slung the bridle reins from both horses over a nearby hitching post. "I'm beginning to think being around you has put some life back into her."

Rose was more than a little surprised by his words. "Oh, I wouldn't go so far as to say that. Emily hardly knows me."

"It doesn't take Emily long to form an opinion about people. She makes friends much faster than I do."

Intrigued by his comment, she asked, "Do you have many friends around here?"

Pausing by Pie's shoulder, he looked up at Rose. "A few. I lost one of them when your father died."

"Yes. Well, I'm sorry for both of us," she said quietly.

Harlan thought she looked on the verge of exhaustion and he continued to study her face with concern. "Do you need me to help you down from your horse?"

Embarrassed at letting her thoughts stray to him instead of the business at hand, she quickly slung her leg over the back of the saddle.

"No," she said to him. "I can make it."

Rose stepped down from the saddle. But as soon as her feet touched the ground, her knees immediately threatened to buckle. Panicked by the weakness and the weird tilting in her head, Rose grabbed for the nearest thing to her, which turned out to be the stirrup, and clung to it desperately.

"Rose?" Suddenly he was right behind her and his hands came around her waist. "What's wrong?"

She dropped her head forward but it didn't seem to help. Everything was whirling like a slow waltz. "I'm...feeling sorta...punchy."

With one hand on her forehead, Harlan pulled her back against his chest. "Close your eyes and take a few deep breaths," he said against her ear. "Don't worry. I won't let you fall."

She did as he instructed and quickly felt her strength begin to return. After a few moments she said, "I'm not going to faint."

"Good."

"You can let me go now."

"I don't think so," he murmured.

Suddenly Rose's heart began to pound as she became

aware of his rock-hard body pressed against the back of hers, the feel of his warm fingers on her waist and forehead.

"Why?" she asked in a voice gone hoarse.

Slowly he turned her in his arms until she was facing him. "Because I'm going to kiss you."

Her senses had gone completely fuzzy. Not from exhaustion, but from the sheer impact of being in his arms. "I don't want you to kiss me."

Harlan grinned and all at once he felt that nothing else mattered except touching her, tasting her. He knew it was crazy and he knew he'd probably hate himself tomorrow. But at this very moment he couldn't resist her.

"How do you know you don't want me to kiss you?"

Hoping it would clear her thinking, she sucked in a deep breath. "Because you're a man."

His grin deepened. "Yeah," he whispered and his brown eyes glinted down at her. "Thank God you came along and reminded me of that."

She needed to shake her head, to get the word *no* past her lips. But before she could do either one, his lips swooped down and covered hers. Stunned by the intimate contact, Rose stiffened and brought her hands up to push him away. But by the time her palms landed against his shoulders, she'd forgotten her intentions.

His kiss was like rich whiskey, hot, potent and totally intoxicating. If she didn't tear her mouth away from his, she'd soon be drunk. But how could she, when all she really wanted was to go on kissing him forever?

Chapter Four

It was Harlan who finally stepped back, separating the warm fusion of their lips. For a moment Rose hardly knew where they were or why. She was breathless and quivering and too stunned for words of any sort.

"I'm sorry, Rose."

She forced her eyes to open and look at him. His mouth was grim but the desire to kiss it again was still with her and she wondered faintly if all the pressure she'd been under lately had finally caused her to crack.

"I took advantage of you at a weak moment," he went on. "It was unfair of me. Not to mention ungentlemanly."

What was unfair, Rose thought, was this warm ache he'd created inside her, then left her with no way to soothe it.

Numbly, she pulled away from his hold and turned toward Pie. "There's no need for you to apologize," she said in a voice that sounded strangely unlike her own. "It was just a kiss."

Just a kiss? It hadn't seemed so to Harlan. His head was still muddled from the feel of her in his arms. And he suspected Rose was just as shaken as he. She just didn't want him to know.

"Maybe so," he began slowly, "but I don't normally go around kissing swooning women."

No, it was the other way around, Rose thought. He kissed and then the swooning began. But she wasn't going to say such a thing to him. She didn't want to talk about what had just happened between them. She didn't want to think about it, either. She simply wanted to go home and forget about Harlan. For as long as she could.

"I don't go around kissing men of any kind," she told him. "So we're even."

Without waiting for a reply she reached to unbuckle the back cinch on Pie's saddle. Harlan knew she wanted to end the matter and the more he thought about it the more he knew it would be wise to follow her wishes. One stolen kiss between them was more than enough.

"Go ahead and unsaddle Pie completely," he told her. "I want you to leave him here tonight."

The abrupt change of subject brought her head back around to him. "Why?"

"He's exhausted. He doesn't need another long ride in the stock trailer. I have plenty of room to pen him separately from my horses. He can roll and eat and rest and you won't have to worry about him."

Rose was too tired to argue with him. Besides, she had no intention of using Pie tomorrow. Not after the work he'd given her today.

"Very well. I'll come pick him up tomorrow after lunch."

"No. I have to go into Ruidoso tomorrow anyway. I'll drop him by the Bar M for you."

She turned back to her horse and quickly slid the saddle from his sweaty withers. "There's no need for you to go to that much trouble."

"It's not nearly as much as you've done for me today."

His words came out softly and Rose's hand paused on Pie's shoulder. So he thought she was doing all this for him. But she wasn't. She was doing it for herself, her family and her home. Or was she?

Minutes later, after they'd tended the horses, Harlan and Rose walked to the house. They found Emily in the kitchen setting the small Formica table. The smell of baking pizza filled the warm room.

Harlan showed Rose to the bathroom, then left her in the small room with its blue tiled walls and white fixtures.

Quickly she filled the basin, soaped her arms and face, then rinsed the suds and loosened grime away with cool water. While she dabbed herself dry with a clean towel, she glanced in the medicine chest mirror.

She was pale, and dark crescents of fatigue shadowed her eyes. Most of her hair had come loose from its French braid and was now curling about her face and shoulders in disarray.

She leaned closer to the mirror and touched a fingertip to her lips. Harlan had kissed her. She was still amazed that he'd done such a thing. She couldn't imagine that he might actually be attracted to her. He couldn't really want her in the way a man wants a woman. Her mind refused to believe it.

Back out in the kitchen, she found Emily struggling to cut up a salad. Rose quelled the urge to take the paring knife from the teenager and dice the tomato herself. Emily would never learn to do things in the kitchen if someone else did them for her.

"What can I do to help?" Rose asked while noticing that Harlan was nowhere in sight.

Dropping the knife, Emily took Rose by the arm and gently guided her to a chair. "Just sit. Daddy said you were feeling a little faint. Are you okay now?"

"I'm fine," Rose assured the girl, then wondered what Emily would think if she knew her father had kissed her. Would she be jealous, resentful? It didn't matter, Rose told herself. Nothing else was going to happen between herself and Harlan Hamilton. "Besides, I'm not used to just sitting down while people around me work. Let me ice the glasses or something."

Returning to the salad makings, Emily shook her head. "Daddy said not to let you do anything. If he comes back in here and finds you on your feet, we'll both be in for it."

Rose couldn't remember the last time anyone had insisted she rest. Her family knew she pushed herself to the point of exhaustion. But so did the rest of her family. Rest was a luxury none of them could afford.

Leaning back in the chair, Rose pushed the dust-coated strands of hair away from her face. "Do you like to cook?" she asked Emily.

The girl shook her head. "Not really. Maybe I would if I knew more about it. But Daddy doesn't cook much either, so he's only taught me a few things. Like scrambling eggs and things like that. Do you know how to cook?"

Rose thought back to the days when she'd been Emily's age. Her mother, Lola, had been a very gentle, feminine woman who'd enjoyed doing all the traditional things like cooking and sewing. She'd insisted her daughters learn as much about homemaking as possible. Justine had always pointed out that she was going to be a nurse and therefore didn't need to know how to make a pair of curtains or bake a pan of biscuits. Chloe, the tomboy of the three, had argued with their mother that making a good enchilada wasn't going to win her a race at Ruidoso Downs. But Rose had been different. She'd enjoyed spending time in the kitchen or sewing room with their mother. Now that Lola was gone from their lives, those times were some of Rose's most precious memories.

"Yes, I like to cook," she told Emily. "I help my Aunt Kitty prepare as many meals as I can."

"Your aunt lives with you?"

Rose's legs were aching. She stretched them beneath the table and rubbed her palms against her thighs. "Yes. She came to stay on the ranch when my mother became ill. They were sisters and very close. After Mother died, she decided she needed all of us as much as we needed her."

"That must be nice. We don't have any relatives around here." Emily dumped the diced tomato into a bowl of torn lettuce and placed it in the center of the table. "Some of my friends tell me I'm lucky because I don't have to sit through boring visits from cousins and aunts and uncles. But I don't think I'm so lucky. I think they are and they just don't know it."

Rose watched the girl go back to the cabinets and quickly take down three bottle green glasses and fill them with crushed ice from an upright freezer. "Do you think you'd rather live back in east Texas? I imagine you have relatives there."

Emily shrugged. "I'd rather live here. I don't remember much about our other place, except that there were lots of trees and grass and it got really hot in the summer."

Rose smiled. "It gets pretty warm here, too."

Footsteps sounded behind her. Rose glanced around to see Harlan entering the kitchen. He'd changed his denim shirt and was now wearing a faded red T-shirt. His dark hair was damp and slicked back from his face. The very maleness of him made something inside Rose quiver with anticipation.

Harlan's gaze met Rose's and lingered for a moment, then moved on to his daughter. "Is it ready? I don't know about you two, but I'm starving."

Before Emily could reply, the timer on the oven began to buzz. Harlan walked over and picked up a pot holder from the cabinet counter. Emily swiftly plucked it from his hands.

"I'm cooking the meal tonight, Daddy. You sit down by Rose and let me do the serving."

With a wry smile, he pulled out a chair directly across from Rose. "Feeling better?"

Rose didn't know if she was feeling better, but she was quite certain she'd never feel the same after this night. Her head was still reeling from that kiss he'd given her and she desperately hoped her shaken emotions didn't show on her face.

"I'm okay."

Her eyes briefly met his, then skittered away to the opposite end of the room. Harlan knew she was probably feeling awkward about their kiss. But hell, he was feeling pretty foolish himself. He hadn't kissed a woman since his wife had died. He hadn't wanted to. Until now. Until Rose.

"You worked too hard today," he said, unaware that his voice had softened.

He sounded truly concerned for her and Rose found it impossible to stop her heart from warming toward him. He had problems of his own. He didn't have to care about her. But he seemed to anyway. Or was she only seeing things that didn't exist? "I didn't work any harder than you or Emily," she countered.

"Emily has the stamina of youth, and I'm a man."

Her eyes drifted back to his face and her heart gave a sudden lurch. This sexy man with his dark hair and brown eyes had kissed her tenderly, passionately and for a brief few moments she'd actually felt like a woman desired. And that was a new and scary feeling for Rose.

"I'm not a weak woman. It's just that—the heat has been so bad and the past couple of weeks I've rarely had time to draw a good breath."

Emily placed the pizza, which she'd already cut into

slices, on the table, then took a seat down from the adults. "Rose, I'd be glad to come over to your place and help. Couldn't I, Daddy?"

Surprise dropped Harlan's jaw while Rose shifted awkwardly in her seat.

"That's...very sweet of you to offer, Emily, but I wouldn't dream of pulling you away from your father. I'm sure he has more than enough for you to do around here."

"If Daddy has a lot of work around here, he hires a man to help him. Most of the time in the summer, I just sit around the house. Bored."

Rose glanced at Harlan. He was staring at his daughter, and if the frown on his face was anything to go by, he wasn't at all pleased.

"I'm touched by your offer, Emily. But it wouldn't be fair to you or your father if you worked with me on the Bar M," Rose said, then felt perfectly awful as a crestfallen look settled over Emily's young face. "I mean, I couldn't pay you anything. And I certainly couldn't let you work for nothing."

Harlan took a piece of the pizza, then motioned for Rose to help herself. "I don't think my daughter expects to be paid. Do you, Emily?"

The teenager shook her head emphatically. "No. But if you'd rather not have me around, I understand," she told Rose.

But she would be brokenhearted. Even though Emily hadn't spoken the words, Rose could read them on her face. The last thing she wanted to do was to hurt this impressionable girl's feelings.

"Oh, well, it's not a matter of whether I'd want you around. I'd love your company."

Emily's face lighted up like a candle. "You would? You're not just saying that?"

Rose shook her head. "Of course not," she said, then glanced at Harlan. "You're not saying anything."

He shrugged as he studied his daughter, then looked at Rose. "This is between you and Emily."

"Then you wouldn't mind if she came over to the ranch a few days a week?"

So far this summer Emily hadn't shown any interest in finding a job. Of course with the closest town being twenty miles away there wasn't much point in looking. But Harlan intuitively knew this thing with Rose had nothing to do with a job. His daughter simply wanted to be with her new-found friend. And how could he deny her the female companionship she so badly needed?

"No. I wouldn't mind."

Before another word could be said, Emily jumped to her feet and raced around to her father's chair. "Oh Daddy, you're so wonderful! Thank you! Thank you!"

She rained kisses on both sides of his face until he laughingly set her back from him.

"Okay, I get the message. You're willing to slave for Rose and leave your dear old dad with a sinkful of dirty dishes."

"Oh, no! I promise I'll help here at home, too, Daddy," she exclaimed as she hurried back to her seat at the table.

Harlan smiled. It was the first time in a long while he'd seen his daughter excited over anything and it made him very happy.

"I'm just kidding, Emily."

As Rose chewed a bite of pizza, she watched the affectionate exchange between father and daughter. Being from a large family herself, it was hard for Rose to imagine how it must be with just the two of them. To say the least, raising a daughter alone would be daunting. Harlan had done it for six or seven years. She figured most men would have given up long before that and married the first woman they could find to say yes.

"Do you know anything about babies, Emily?" Rose asked.

"Babies? You mean baby animals?"

Rose smiled. "No. I mean baby people."

Emily was suddenly intrigued. "Oh. I've never been around any babies hardly. Why?"

"Because we have twin babies on the ranch. I thought you might enjoy looking after them a bit."

Emily's eyes grew wide. "Babies! Are they yours? Are you married?"

Harlan was looking at her as though she'd just metamorphosed and Rose couldn't stop the hot blush from pouring into her cheeks. Surely he didn't think she'd given birth to the babies! One kiss with him wasn't enough to make her appear that promiscuous!

"No, I'm not married and the babies aren't mine. At least not technically speaking. They're twins and they're eight months old."

"Twin babies! How wonderful!" Emily exclaimed. "I can't wait to see them!"

Emily continued to chatter about the babies and her plans to visit the ranch. In a matter of minutes, the pizza and salad were gone and it was time for Rose to head home.

As she told Emily goodbye and climbed into the pickup with Harlan, she wished his daughter was going with them. She didn't want to be alone with the man for five minutes, much less fifteen or twenty. But she had little choice in the matter.

"I want you to know how grateful I am to you, Rose," Harlan said as they drove away from the ranch onto the dark dirt road.

His unexpected words caused her head to swivel his way.

"Grateful? I can't imagine for what. You loaned Daddy lots of money. You're more than entitled to our water."

Harlan shook his head. "I'm not talking about any of that."

Dear heaven, he wasn't talking about that kiss, was he? She wished he'd forget it. She wished she could wipe it completely from her mind. But how could she, when just sitting here beside him in the dark was making her heart pound?

"Then what—"

"I'm talking about Emily. She's taken to you. And I'm…more than grateful that you didn't push her away tonight."

Rose sagged with relief. She could talk about Emily. She couldn't talk about what had happened between the two of them down by the barn.

"Emily is a lovely child. I wouldn't push her away for any reason."

He sighed. "That's very generous of you. Especially after the rude way she behaved yesterday." He grunted a sound of amused disbelief. "Last night she refused to ride with us to the Bar M and now she can't wait to go. I don't know if I'll ever understand my daughter."

"Maybe it's females in general that you don't understand," she said, then immediately wanted to bite her tongue. What had possessed her to say such a thing to him?

"I don't pretend to try," he said dryly, then cast a curious glance at her. "I know it's none of my business, but those babies you were talking about earlier. Do they belong to one of your sisters? I remember Tomas mentioning one of his daughters having a son, but I don't remember anything about twins."

"That's my sister Justine. She and Roy have a five-year-old son. The twins are—"

She hesitated, then quickly decided there wasn't any

point in keeping the circumstances of the twins a secret from this man. She wasn't ashamed of the twins. Of her father's behavior, certainly. But never the twins. She couldn't love them more.

She went on, "Back earlier in the summer, Justine found the twins on our front porch."

"On your porch," he repeated in disbelief. "That sounds like something in the movies."

Sighing, Rose gazed at the shadowy clumps of sage and choya passing outside the open window. "I know. But it happens to be exactly what happened."

Harlan's mouth tightened to a grim line. "Who would do such a thing to innocent children?"

She glanced at him. "Sheriff Roy Pardee is my brother-in-law and since he's been working on the case, he's pretty much decided it was the mother. She was seen with the twins in Ruidoso on that very same day. It must have been her. But I guess he won't be absolutely sure of that until he tracks her down."

"He hasn't found the mother yet?"

Rose shook her head. "So far she's left a pretty cold trail to follow. But Roy is good at his job and I feel like he'll find her soon."

"Does he know who she is? What about the father?"

"The father is dead," she said flatly.

He slowed the pickup and stared at her. "Dead? How do you know that?"

She swallowed. "Because Tomas, my father, is also the father of the twins."

Harlan couldn't believe it. Tomas had only become a widower late last year. Was Rose telling him the old man had been having an affair?

He stopped the pickup in the middle of the dirt road and killed the motor. "Rose, surely I didn't hear you right.

Tomas, your father, is also the father of the babies left abandoned on your front porch?''

She sighed wearily. The day had been exhausting and she was still feeling like a genuine fool over that kiss. She was hardly in the mood to discuss her father's lack of morals, but since she'd already told him part of the story, she couldn't very well hold back the rest. He'd been a friend to Tomas, he'd lent him money when he needed it. If anyone had the right to know what had happened, she supposed Harlan did.

"For a while we didn't know who or where the twins belonged," she said quietly. "We knew the babies were redheaded like myself and my sisters. And some people even remarked that they resembled us, but we didn't know anyone with twin babies. We thought it was all just coincidence and that someone had randomly chosen the Bar M as a place to drop the babies."

"How did you find out? About your father, I mean," he asked gently.

"I was going through some of the ranch's canceled checks and discovered several my father had written at a certain time each month. All the checks were for a large amount and the name of the payee had been left blank. And to make things even more suspicious, the endorser never put a name, just a deposit only. But thankfully the number of the account the money was deposited into was stamped on the back. And from that Roy was able to find a name and eventually the birth records of the twins in Las Cruces. Tomas was listed as the father and we have no reason to doubt that. Since the twins have grown over a few more months, they're beginning to look even more like Murdocks."

Harlan couldn't imagine what a shock it must have been for Rose to find out the twins were actually her siblings. Had the whole thing made her hate her father?

"Why do you think Tomas was writing those checks? For child support?"

Rose shrugged. "We don't know for sure. He obviously didn't want us knowing about the twins and since the mother never made any sort of contact with us beforehand, we think she was blackmailing our father—to keep quiet about giving birth to his children."

Harlan's head swung slowly back and forth. "This is all—so incredible. Tomas was a fine man. There were times he offered to help me when I didn't even ask. I can't imagine him getting off on such a wrong track." He looked at Rose and tried to imagine what she'd been coping with these past months. A lesser woman would have already crumbled under the weight, he realized. "I suppose this was why your father came to me for money. The whole thing must have broken him."

Rose leaned her head against the back of the seat. She looked so tired and defeated that Harlan wished he hadn't asked her anything about the babies. Obviously, just talking about it had drained her.

"I shouldn't have asked you," he said after a moment. "It was none of my business."

Rose turned her large gray eyes on him and as he looked into their depths, he could see the pain and worry and exhaustion she was feeling. Harlan suddenly wanted to take her into his arms and rest her head against his shoulder. He wanted to stroke her hair and tell her everything would eventually be all right. But it wasn't his place to comfort her and more than likely she'd be the first one to tell him so.

"I don't feel that way, Harlan. You loaned Daddy money. You're entitled to know what he wanted it for. Besides, I knew if Emily came to the ranch and met the babies, she'd want to know something about them. What shall I tell her?"

Rose's question caused his brows to lift. "What do you mean?"

"Emily is thirteen. She might not understand about an older married man having an affair." She stopped and covered her face with both hands. "What am I saying? I'm twenty-eight and I don't even understand it myself."

She was twenty-eight. Harlan was surprised. She looked much younger. And as far as he knew, she'd never been married. For the life of him, he couldn't figure why. Rose was a lovely, alluring woman. Even under her dusty work clothes and boots he could see that. Did she simply not like men because her father had turned out to be an adulterer? No, he didn't think so. That wouldn't account for all these years she lived a single life. Besides, she'd kissed him and he hadn't tasted a bit of dislike on her lips.

"Whatever Emily asks about the twins, tell her the truth. She's old enough to know that the world isn't always a nice place. And I've tried to teach her that, if they're not careful, people of any age can make bad mistakes."

Rose dropped her hands to her lap, looked at him, and tried her best to smile. "I think—you're a good father, Harlan."

It was the last thing he was expecting her to say. The compliment both surprised and pleased him. "Thank you, Rose. I try."

He started the engine and headed on to the Bar M. For the rest of the drive, Rose closed her eyes and tried to put Harlan out of her thoughts. But that was about as successful as her turning night into day. She owed the man money. That troubled her. But not nearly as much as the unfamiliar feelings stirring inside her. She was letting herself get closer to Harlan. She was even beginning to like him. And that terrified her.

A few minutes later they arrived at the ranch and Rose directed Harlan to circle around to the back of the house.

As soon as he parked at the gate entering the courtyard, Rose reached for the doorhandle.

"Thank you for the lift, Harlan," she said, her eyes fixed safely on her lap. "And don't worry yourself about getting Pie back tomorrow. Just drop him by whenever you have the chance. I'll pay you for whatever feed you give him."

His door opened and she glanced over to see him climbing out to the ground. Bemused, she watched him skirt the front of the cab, then open her door.

"You won't pay me anything for horse feed," he said, then raised his arm toward her. "Put your hand on my arm."

She frowned. "What?"

"Put your hand right here," he ordered while tapping his forearm. "I'm going to walk you to the door."

"That isn't necessary. I'm fine now."

"Maybe so. But this way I'll know you made it to the house without collapsing."

Rose had never collapsed in her life and she certainly didn't want Harlan thinking she was weak. For some foolish reason, she wanted him to see her as a strong, confident woman. Yet he seemed to want her to lean on him and that idea went straight to Rose's heart.

Reaching out, she curled her fingers over his thick forearm. At once, she was struck by the warmth of his skin, the tickle of body hair, the hardness of his muscles.

Her heart lurched, then went into a mad gallop as she slid from the seat to stand beside him.

"I guess I am a little tired," she told him. But she didn't feel it. When she was close to him, touching him, her whole body buzzed with excitement. It didn't make sense.

Except for a faint night-light burning in the kitchen, the back courtyard was dark as the two of them slowly made their way toward the house. As they walked, Harlan was acutely aware of Rose's small hand on his arm. It had been

years since a woman had touched him or needed him in a
physical way. To have Rose leaning on him swelled his
chest with inexplicable emotions.

The night had grown late and nothing was stirring except
a soft breeze whispering in the pines. Rose was very aware
of the quietness as the two of them stepped onto the porch.

"Here you are," he said.

"Yes. Well...good night, Harlan."

His hand closed over hers, preventing Rose from stepping away from him. Her eyes lifted to the shadowy lines
of his face and her heart slowed to a heavy thud, thud.

"Rose, I—" he paused and his fingers pressed her hand
even tighter against his arm. "I just wanted to say
that...when you first told me about your financial problems,
I was skeptical. I knew your father needed money last year,
but I didn't think it was...well, I thought you and your
sisters might be the sort who liked to live—" he broke off
awkwardly.

"Above our means," she finished dryly.

A sheepish expression on his face, he said, "Something
like that. And I feel bad about it now."

She looked down at the toes of their dusty boots. His
were wide and rounded, hers narrow and pointed. They
were very nearly touching. So were their thighs and hips
and the whole idea made it hard for Rose to breathe.

"You shouldn't apologize for that, Harlan. You don't
know me or my sisters, or how we live."

No, he hadn't known much about the Murdock daughters, but he was quickly learning about this one, he thought.
And the more he learned, the more he was drawn to her.

"But I knew your father," he persisted. "At least, I
thought I knew him. It's hard to believe he would have left
his family in such financial trouble."

Rose looked up at him and was surprised to find something like sadness on his face. When Harlan had called

Tomas his friend, he must have truly meant it, Rose thought. "Daddy was only fifty-three. I don't think he planned on dying and leaving things the way he did. I believe he thought he'd eventually make the money back and none of us would ever be aware of his problems."

"He must have been living under a hell of a load," Harlan said thoughtfully.

"I'm sure it's what killed him. The stress of it all. Of course his cigarettes and fondness for Kentucky bourbon didn't help matters."

Tomas Murdock had liked to play the horses. Harlan had been aware of that. But apparently the older man's playing hadn't stopped at just horses. Now Rose and her sisters were paying for his sins. It wasn't fair, or right. But what could Harlan do about it?

"I'm sorry, Rose. Really sorry."

She closed her eyes and as Harlan studied her pale face, it was all he could do not to crush her against his chest and bury his face in her hair. The urge didn't make sense to Harlan. After the death of his wife, he'd vowed never to marry or even allow himself to love again. So why was this woman making him feel things he didn't want to feel?

"I didn't tell you all this to gain your sympathy," she murmured.

"No. But I'm glad you did," he said softly.

Her eyes fluttered open just in time to see his face drawing near. Her mouth opened in surprise but she didn't have time to get the word *no* past her lips. Suddenly he was kissing her. Again.

Rose couldn't help herself. She clung to him, tasted him, then sighed when he finally lifted his head and gently trailed his finger down her cheek.

"Good night, Rose."

Too shaken to speak, Rose watched him disappear into the darkness.

"Good night, Harlan," she whispered brokenly.

Chapter Five

A few moments later Rose pulled herself together and went into the house. All was quiet as she walked through the dark living room, then down the hallway toward her bedroom.

"Rose?"

The whispered sound of her name had Rose pausing, then glancing in the open doorway of the nursery. A soft night-light illuminated Chloe's silhouette.

"Yes, it's me. Are they both asleep?" she asked as she tiptoed into the twins' room.

Chloe turned away from the white wooden cribs. "I just put them down. I think they crawled across the living room thirty times before they finally wore down."

"They like being mobile," Rose said with a weary smile. "Just wait until they start walking."

Chloe chuckled softly. "Look out, Aunt Kitty. She'll probably drop ten pounds."

"By then I expect we'll have to hire someone to help her. Aunt Kitty might be young and agile for her sixty-two years, but chasing after two toddlers would be hard on a woman of any age.''

Chloe glanced over her shoulder at the sleeping babies. ''I know. I just hope by then we can come up with the money for extra help.'' She looked back at her sister. ''Speaking of help, where have you been?''

Out on the porch kissing our neighbor, Rose thought wildly. Aloud she said, ''Harlan just brought me home. It was dark by the time we finished moving the cattle. And then his daughter wanted me to stay and eat pizza.''

Chloe's brows shot up. ''And you did?''

Rose took Chloe by the shoulder and guided her out of the nursery. ''It would have been unneighborly to have refused, don't you think?''

She headed down the hallway to her bedroom and Chloe walked along with her.

''I don't know about that. But it surprises me that you stayed to have supper with someone you hardly know. Especially when you told me last night that Harlan—what was it?'' She thoughtfully tapped a finger against her chin. ''He bothered you.''

Rose spread her hands in a helpless gesture. ''Well, he does bother me.'' Dear Lord, he did more than bother her, she thought, he'd taken total control of her senses. ''But Emily was a big help moving the cattle today and she practically begged me to stay and eat.''

''Hmm,'' Chloe mused aloud, ''you must like the girl.''

Rose entered her bedroom with Chloe still close on her heels. ''I do. Her mother has been dead since she was a little thing and it's just been her and her daddy ever since.''

''How sad for her.''

''Very.''

''And sad for Mr. Hamilton, too,'' Chloe added.

Rose tossed her hat onto a stuffed armchair, then in spite

of her dusty clothes and boots, sank wearily onto the bed. "Losing a spouse would be more than sad."

"I wonder why he's never married again? I'm sure there're plenty of women out there who'd jump at the chance to be his wife."

Rose shot her sister an annoyed look. "What makes you say that? You don't even know the man."

"I've seen him around before. He's quite a man."

"You know that just by looking at him?" Rose asked dryly.

"I talked to the man once when he was visiting Daddy. He's mighty easy on the eyes and he has one of those drawls that give you goose bumps on the inside."

So Rose wasn't by herself when it came to being affected by Harlan Hamilton's charms, she thought. "So why didn't you flirt with him? He might have decided to change his single status."

Chloe's mouth fell open. "Rose! I can't believe you said that to me!"

Rose couldn't believe it, either. But she hadn't been herself these past two days. Maybe the drought and heat and work had all finally gotten to her. She had to think that's all it was.

Lying back against the pillows, Rose closed her eyes. "Why? You just said the man was very attractive. And you're young and beautiful and single."

Groaning, Chloe sat down on the edge of the bed. "My horses don't allow me any time for romance. And even if I wasn't busy with them, I'm not so sure I could get interested in any man. Not after the things Daddy did to mother and us. Anyway," she added with a dismissive wave of her hand, "Mr. Hamilton is probably ten years my senior."

Rose opened her eyes. "I told Harlan about Daddy and the twins."

For a second time Chloe's jaw dropped with shock. "You told him! All of it?"

Rose nodded. "I felt we owed it to him. He lent Daddy all that money. And you and I both know what he did with it. Every cent was given to Belinda Waller."

"That's true enough," Chloe agreed with a grimace. "But I can't imagine you sharing such a private thing with Harlan Hamilton."

"Whether we like it or not, the man is a part of our lives now, Chloe. At least until we're able to pay him back. But aside from all that, his daughter Emily is going to be coming over here to the ranch from time to time. She needed to know and understand how the twins came to be here with us."

Chloe's brows shot up. "His daughter is going to be coming here? Why?"

"She plans on helping me with whatever I need to get done."

"You can't pay her!"

A wan little smile curved Rose's lips. "She doesn't want pay. She wants companionship. I hope you'll be nice to her."

Chloe appeared properly offended by her sister's remark. "I'm nice to everyone."

Rose gave her younger sister a skeptical glance.

"Okay, almost everyone," Chloe conceded, then pressed her hand over Rose's. "It's getting late and you look beat. Would you like me to run you a bath?"

"I don't know that I have enough strength for a bath. I think I'll do well just to get these clothes off."

"Oh Rose," Chloe scolded, "you can't keep this up. You can't do the work of five or six men. It's killing you!"

Rose gave her sister a weary, lopsided smile. "Look who's talking."

Chloe shook her head. "My work is confined to the stable. You're trying to oversee thousands of acres!"

"And you're trying to help Aunt Kitty with the twins. Believe me, Chloe, it all equals out. Besides, today was out of the ordinary."

"Yeah, thanks to Mr. Hamilton." She got up from the bed and reached for Rose's boots. As she tugged them off she said, "I hope this keeps the man satisfied for a while. But I'm afraid he's eventually going to want more from us Murdocks than just water for his cattle."

Rose sighed and wiggled her bare toes. "If he does, we'll just have to try to give it to him. I don't know what else we could do."

Chloe snorted. "I'll tell you something, Rose, I'll be damn glad when we get ourselves out of this mess. I don't like being at the mercy of any man's whims. When it all boils down to the bottom of the pot, a man is going to take care of his wants first and to hell with anybody else."

Rose made a tsking noise with her tongue. "You're becoming jaded, Chloe."

"I've got a right to." She sniffed as she gave the belt on her bathrobe a hard jerk. "Just like you've got a right to despise men. After what Peter did to you, it's a wonder you didn't want to go into a convent!"

"Dear Lord, Chloe, I have enough on my mind without you bringing him up."

Chloe heaved out a breath, then shook her head with regret. "You're right. I'm sorry, Rose. It's just that I get so angry when I think about everything that's happened." Her expression softening, she bent down and kissed her sister's cheek. "Let's go to bed and try to forget about all of it. At least for tonight."

"That's exactly what I'm going to do. Good night, sis."

* * *

More than an hour later Rose lay in her bed, exhausted yet still wide awake. No matter how hard she tried to quiet her mind, it continued to spin. And it was all Harlan's fault. He should have never kissed her in the first place, much less a second time!

Her fingers drifted to her lips as the taste of him lingered in her thoughts. After all these years, she'd never dreamed that a man's kiss or touch would affect her like this. She was frigid and had been ever since her one and only engagement had ended eight years ago.

She'd met Peter during her second year of college at Eastern New Mexico State. He'd been blond and good-looking. Flirty and outgoing. The exact opposite of Rose's quiet personality. She supposed the difference was what had first attracted her to him. Yet beneath his looks and personality, he'd been a dedicated student working toward a degree in medicine. In short, he'd been everything a young woman looked for in a fiancé and for a while Rose was blissfully dreaming of their future together.

With a little groan, she raised herself up in the bed and pushed her fingers through her tangled hair. She didn't want to think about the pain she'd endured at Peter's hands. But tonight she couldn't seem to turn off her memories or the old fears that had stayed with her all these years.

She supposed in some ways, she still blamed herself for their tragic breakup. Peter had wanted sex from her and she'd been too young and innocent to give in before their marriage. The more he'd demanded, the more she'd resisted until it finally reached a point where their relationship was nothing but one big fight about sex.

The night Rose finally told Peter it was over between them, he'd gone into a rage. Once it was all over she'd been badly beaten and very nearly raped. The experience had frozen her, robbed her of her dreams of a loving husband and children.

But now Harlan had come along and kissed her as though

it had been a perfectly normal thing to do. And she'd responded as though she was a perfectly normal woman. But she wasn't. She had to remember that. She had to remember she would never be a lover, a wife, a mother.

For the first time in weeks, Rose slept late the next morning. Although for most people, six-thirty would still be regarded as early, she considered it horribly lazy to lie in bed until after daylight.

She'd just showered and dressed in a clean pair of jeans and a pale blue shirt when she heard unfamiliar voices coming from the kitchen.

Quickly tying her hair back with a blue scarf, she hurried from her bedroom. Once she reached the open doorway to the kitchen, she came to an abrupt halt.

Harlan and Emily were sitting at the breakfast table and from the looks of things, Kitty had already served him a cup of coffee and a slice of cherry pie.

"Oh, there you are, Rose," the older woman said as she spotted her niece. "I was just about to call you and let you know we have company this morning."

"You shouldn't consider us company, Kitty," Harlan said as easily as if he'd known her for years.

Kitty smiled at him. "Then I'll call you neighbors."

His attention turned to Rose and a flush of heat filled her cheeks as she returned his gaze. She'd thought about the man half the night. To see him this morning, his face freshly shaven, his dark hair gleaming damply against his head was very disconcerting.

"Good morning, Rose."

She nodded a greeting to him, then turned to Emily. "Good morning, Emily. You're up early."

"I wanted to come with Daddy when he dropped off your horse. Will it be all right if I stay and help you today?"

"Emily," Harlan said to his daughter, "give Rose a chance to catch her breath. As tired as she was last night, she's probably not going to do any work today."

Kitty laughed with disbelief. "Rose not work? That'll be the day!"

Ignoring her aunt's comment, Rose took a seat across from Emily. "Of course it will be all right for you to stay. I have a pen of heifers that need to be tagged and vaccinated."

"And then what?" Emily asked eagerly.

Rose smiled at the girl's enthusiasm. "Oh, don't worry. I'm sure we'll find plenty to do," she said, then darted a look at Harlan. She could see appreciation in his eyes and it filled her with a strange warmness. He obviously wanted his daughter to be happy and that in itself endeared the man to her.

"Are you going to eat breakfast now, Rose?" Kitty asked as she walked over to the cookstove. "I've got plenty of pancake batter left."

Before Rose could reply, two loud wails sounded from the nursery down the hall.

"The twins are awake," Kitty stated the obvious. "Would you go get them, Rose, while I make your breakfast?"

Rose excused herself and hurried down to the nursery. After quickly changing both babies' wet diapers, she tucked Adam in the crook of her arm, then circled her other arm securely around Anna.

A few moments later when she entered the kitchen carrying both babies, Emily squealed with delight. "Oh, Daddy, look! Look how cute they are!"

The babies did resemble Rose and her sisters. And as Harlan gazed at the three of them, it was easy for him to imagine Rose as a mother, a baby of her own cradled in her arms. She was meant to love a man, a child. He could easily see that about her. But apparently she couldn't see it herself.

"May I hold one, Rose? I'll be really careful!" Emily very nearly begged.

"Sure you may. I'll let you hold Anna. She's not quite as rowdy as her brother, Adam."

Rose gently eased the baby girl down onto Emily's lap. Anna immediately looked up at the teenager, then let out a loud, cooing laugh which prompted a giggle from Emily.

"Why don't you give rowdy Adam to me?" Harlan spoke up. "It's been a long time since I've held a baby, but I think I can handle him."

Trying not to appear surprised, Rose handed Adam over to him. And as she watched him stand the baby up against his broad chest, it was easy to see he hadn't forgotten how to be a daddy to an infant.

"Here you go, honey," Kitty said to Rose as she plunked down a plate of hot pancakes. "You'd better eat them while we've got two baby-sitters."

Rose murmured her thanks then took a seat and dug into her breakfast.

Across the table Emily gushed over the twins. "Gosh, they look so much alike! Do they cry a lot? Are they big enough to eat food?"

"They don't cry too much," Kitty answered as she pushed a cup of coffee at Rose, then sat down with a mug of her own.

"I imagine they can eat soft things," Harlan told his daughter, then with the tip of his forefinger explored Adam's gums. The baby immediately chomped down and Harlan let out a husky laugh. "Yeah, feels like he's got a couple of teeth."

Emily darted a curious look at her father. "I didn't know you knew anything about babies, Daddy."

He chuckled again. "I know you consider yourself grown-up now. But you were once my baby."

His baby. Rose didn't know why those two words should sound so sweet to her. But they did. She could easily imagine Harlan with another baby. A brother or sister to Emily. Had he ever longed for another child? she wondered. Did he ever want to be that close to another woman again?

Rose mentally shook herself. What was she doing? What was she thinking? The first evening she'd met Harlan he'd made it quite clear he never wanted to get married again. But making love to a woman didn't necessarily always mean marrying her, she thought. Peter had certainly taught her that much. Then her father had come along and reiterated the fact.

"This little guy is going to be stocky like Tomas," Harlan commented, as he balanced the boy on his thigh.

Kitty swiftly glanced at him. "You know Tomas is the twins' father?"

He nodded. "Rose told me."

"Did the mother really leave them on the porch?" Emily asked. "How could she do that?"

"We don't know who left them for sure, honey," Kitty answered. "The sheriff hasn't been able to find her. When he does maybe we'll get some answers."

"Well," Harlan said as he rose to his feet. "Thank you for the pie, Kitty. I guess I'd better turn this fella over to you and head on to town." He handed the baby to Kitty, then walked to the door.

Rose kept her eyes firmly on her plate and told herself not to be disappointed that he was leaving. She had work to do. She couldn't spend her time visiting with Harlan. It was crazy of her to even want to.

"Rose, if you'll tell me where to put your horse, I'll unload him from the trailer."

There were three bites left on her plate. She took one more, then stood. "I'll show you."

"When are you coming back to get me, Daddy?" Emily asked him.

"Whenever Rose tells me."

Rose looked from father to daughter and back again. "I'll drive Emily home later this evening," she told him.

From the corner of her eye, Rose could see Kitty raise her brows. No doubt her aunt was wondering what was going on with her and the Hamiltons. But there wasn't anything going on. Not really, she argued with herself. She was simply trying to help a lonely teenage girl. And her father. That was all.

"Okay! I'll see you later, Daddy." Emily blew him a kiss over Anna's bright curly head.

Harlan waved goodbye to his daughter, then went on out the door. Rose followed and the two of them walked slowly through the courtyard. The morning was warm, the sky vibrant blue with not one cloud to be found. Kitty had already turned a sprinkler on the geraniums and marigolds, bordering the walkway. The lack of rain was unusual for this time of the year. But then these past few months of Rose's life had been very unusual. A searing drought was merely one more thing to add to her list of problems.

"I'm afraid you've started something," Harlan said. "Emily is going to want to come over here every day."

"Don't worry about it, Harlan. The novelty of me and my family will wear off after a while. Until then, she's perfectly welcome to come every day if she wants. To be honest, we'll be grateful for any help she can give us. I'm just sorry we can't pay her. Maybe later when...things get better we can write her a nice check."

By now they had reached the gate leading outside. Harlan reached over and put his hand on Rose's forearm. She lifted questioning eyes to his face.

"Rose, I wish you wouldn't keep bringing up the subject of money. I'd like to think that money isn't the only thing between us."

Her heart began to pound. Heat poured through her body and tinged her cheeks a dusky pink. "But there isn't anything else between us."

His fingers tightened ever so slightly on her arm as he studied her face. "That isn't true. You're not being kind to Emily just because you owe me money."

Rose looked properly offended. "Of course not!"

He grinned. "And you didn't help me with the cattle yesterday, simply because you felt you owed it to me. Did you?"

Her gaze moved from his face to the mountains looming behind him. "Well, no. You needed help and I was there. That's all there was to it."

"Then I guess you kissed me because you're indebted to me."

Her eyes jerked back to his face. "*I* kissed *you?*"

"Well, I wasn't entirely alone in the matter."

Rose was mortified. And though she was normally very slow to anger, at this moment she could feel her temper inching upward. "If you were a gentleman you wouldn't discuss such…things with me! You wouldn't have kissed me in the first place. Now you're trying to act as though I liked it!"

Her agitation only served to deepen the grin on his face. "You did like it, Rose. Who are you trying to fool? Yourself?"

Her expression turned to an accusing glare. "You told me you were going to forget all about it. You said it wouldn't happen again. You lied on both counts!"

He stepped closer and curled his strong fingers around both her shoulders. Rose's heart leaped to a frantic pace.

"I didn't lie," he murmured as his face drew within a

mere inch of hers. "I tried to forget about kissing you. I wanted to forget it. And I damn well didn't plan on it happening again. But something about you..."

He shook his head and Rose didn't know if it was frustration, regret or downright anger she saw on his face.

"I haven't done anything to encourage you, Harlan. I don't—you're the first man who's gotten near me in years. And I'm still not sure why I let it happen. But I do know I have no intention of having any sort of physical relationship with you. It's out of the question!"

Her lips were quivering and her gray eyes had grown dark and wide. She looked almost afraid of him and Harlan wondered how she could possibly feel so threatened by him and two little kisses. Dear Lord, didn't she know he would never want to hurt her for any reason?

"Rose, I'm not asking you to have a physical relationship with me."

Her face burned with humiliation. "Then what do you want from me? Other than money?"

He wanted far more than he should, Harlan thought. He wanted to kiss her, hold her, make love to her. He simply wanted to be with her. But she obviously didn't want to hear such a thing from him. And he wasn't at all sure he wanted to confess such a thing to her.

Lifting his hand from her shoulder, he gently traced his fingertips over her reddened cheek. "There you go again. Does everything always come down to money with you?"

Rose didn't know if the sigh slipping past her lips was because of his touch or because she was suddenly ashamed of herself. She'd forgotten how to be a real woman. Or maybe she'd never been one, she thought sadly.

"No," she answered, her gaze dropping to the front of his chambray work shirt. "I guess...since all this has happened with Daddy, money has become something I have to think about all the time. Especially now that I know we owe you—''

His fingertips moved over her lips and Rose's insides began to quiver. She didn't understand what this man had done to her, but for some reason her body had become a traitor to her closely guarded heart. Each time he touched her, it surged with desire. Every time she looked at him, she wanted to get closer, to hear his voice and feel the roughness of his hands on her skin.

''I want to forget all about your daddy's loan for right now, Rose. I'm not going anywhere. And you're not going anywhere. I'm not worried about the money. I know I'll eventually be paid back.''

Her eyes lifted to his. ''How can you be so sure? It turned out that Daddy's word didn't stand for much. If I were you, I wouldn't trust his daughter one little bit.''

One corner of his mouth curved upward. ''You're not a thief, Rose.''

No, she was a frigid woman who was rapidly thawing and the whole idea terrified her far more than money, or droughts, or losing the Bar M.

''No, I'm not a thief. But I don't know when I'll ever be able to repay you,'' she said gravely.

His fingers pushed through her silky hair, then lingered on the blue scarf. ''Right now, I only want you to be my friend. Can you give me that much?''

She'd already given him that and much, much more. He just didn't know it yet.

His brown eyes were warm and Rose felt them drawing her ever closer to him. ''I'll be your friend, Harlan. But don't ask me for more.''

He swallowed as the urge to kiss her welled up in him. ''Being just your friend might turn out to be a hard thing to do, Rose.''

She drew in a bracing breath and turned away from him. "Living is a hard thing to do, Harlan. Haven't you figured that out yet?"

Chapter Six

"I really liked your sister and your aunt," Emily said later that evening as Rose drove toward the Hamilton ranch house.

Rose glanced over at Harlan's daughter, who was riding with her elbow stuck out the pickup window. "I'm glad. They liked you very much."

Emily's dust-smeared face was wreathed in smiles and if Rose hadn't been driving, she would have been sorely tempted to hug the girl and kiss both her cheeks. Emily had been a great help to her, Kitty and even Chloe. Rose knew she had to be tired, yet she seemed to be riding on a happy cloud.

"Do you really think so?"

"I sure do."

Emily sighed wistfully. "It must be so wonderful having a family like yours." She glanced curiously at Rose. "Were you happy when you found out the twins were your brother and sister?"

Rose's first reaction had been pure shock. She couldn't

believe her father had betrayed her mother in such a way. And keeping the twins' existence from his daughters had been an outrageous lie in itself. Yet when Rose looked at the twins she felt nothing but fierce, protective love. They were her siblings. They were as innocent in the matter as she, Justine, and Chloe. Maybe even more so because they were helpless babies, who'd been tossed away by their mother like dirty rags in the trash.

"I was very happy," she told Emily. "And I'll be even happier once I know we have the legal right to keep them permanently."

Emily thought about this for a moment. "You know, I think it's better not to have a mother at all, than to have one who didn't want you. Daddy says my mother loved me very much."

"I'm sure she did."

"I used to think about her a lot. But now it's not so easy." Her young face full of guilt, she glanced at Rose. "Sometimes it's hard for me to remember exactly what she looked like. And that makes me feel bad."

Rose's heart was suddenly aching for Harlan's daughter. "You shouldn't feel bad about that, Emily. Everyone's memories dim over time and you were very young when you lost your mother."

Emily shook her head. "But I don't want to forget her, Rose. I want to remember how she smelled, the way she used to rub my feet before she put on my shoes, and how she always baked cookies for me on Saturdays. I want to remember everything I can about her."

Rose reached over and squeezed Emily's small hand. "I promise you won't ever forget your mother, Emily. Because she'll always be in here." She tapped the region of her own heart. "That's where memories of my mother live. So do yours."

Emily shrugged. "I guess you're right. But sometimes I wish—"

She broke off and Rose could see the girl wasn't entirely comfortable with what she'd been about to say.

"You wish what?"

The guilt was back on Emily's face again. Yet this time there was also a wistful yearning, a longing in her blue eyes that nearly broke Rose's heart.

"I wish," she said lowly, "that Daddy would marry again so I could have a mother who was really with me. And I could have brothers and sisters and we could all be one big family. Is that selfish of me, Rose?"

Not too many evenings ago, Harlan had more or less asked Rose the very same question in reverse. Was it selfish of him not to marry and provide Emily with a much needed mother? Rose hadn't really known how to answer him. Under the circumstances, she was a poor soul to be dealing out opinions on love and marriage. Yet as for Emily's question, the answer was easy.

"You're not being selfish to want those things, Emily. You're being normal and human." She geared the truck even lower as they neared a rough spot in the road. Once she maneuvered it, she looked over at the teenager. "Have you told your father your feelings about this?"

"No," she said glumly. "I've heard him tell his friends he doesn't ever want to get married again. He says he couldn't go through losing another wife."

Rose patted Emily's bare arm. "Your father has been through a lot of pain. Try to remember that when you get frustrated with him. In any case, he loves you a lot."

Emily didn't say anything for a moment, but then a small smile gradually touched her face. "I know. And all my friends think Daddy is a real hunk." She twisted her head toward Rose. "Do you think he's a hunk, Rose?"

Rose carefully cleared her throat. Where was Emily's

mind headed with this? she wondered. "Harlan is a—nice-looking man," she quietly agreed.

Emily didn't appear put off by her lukewarm answer. Rather, she folded her arms and grinned smugly. "Karen, she's a friend of mine at school, says her mother thinks Daddy is really sexy. And Karen says her mom would really like a date with Daddy."

"Oh. Well, I hope this woman is single," was all Rose could think to say.

Emily waved her hand through the hot air. "She's divorced. But if she thinks my dad is a hunk and you do, too, then it shouldn't be all that hard for him to find a woman to marry him. If he really started looking. What do you think?"

He wouldn't even have to look, Rose thought. If he'd stand still long enough, the women would flock around him like hens to a rooster.

"I think you'd better let your father handle his own romantic aspirations."

Emily frowned. "Well, it doesn't hurt for me to dream," she said with a hopeful sigh.

No, dreaming for a family didn't hurt, Rose supposed. She'd done it for the past eight years.

A few moments later, Rose parked the truck in front of the house and left the engine idling.

"Aren't you going to come in for a while?" Emily asked as she slid to the ground.

Rose shook her head. "Maybe next time. Kitty will be starting supper soon and she'll need someone to watch the twins."

Emily nodded that she understood. "Okay. I'll see you in the morning."

She waved goodbye. Rose waved back, then reversed the truck around to head toward home. Just as she was about to drive away, she glanced in the rearview mirror and spotted Harlan walking quickly up from the barn toward her truck.

She'd hoped to get away without having to speak to him. He'd already wreaked enough havoc on her state of mind for one day. But he obviously knew she'd seen him, so there was little for her to do but find out what he wanted.

Shoving the gearshift in Neutral, she waited for him to approach her open window. Once he did, she said nothing, just looked at him with raised brows.

"I wanted to thank you for bringing Emily home. I know you're busy and it's a nuisance for you to drive all this way."

No one had ever confounded her thinking the way this man seemed to. He genuinely appreciated everything that she had done for him and Emily. His gratitude was in his voice and on his face and she couldn't help feeling pleased. Even a bit needed. Yet now that he'd more or less admitted that he was attracted to her, she wanted to run from him as fast as her legs could travel.

"It's no problem. Emily was a great help to me today and I enjoyed her company."

Resting his forearms on the open window of the truck, he studied her with a slow sweep of his brown eyes. A part of Rose wanted to jerk the gearshift in first and step on the gas. The other part of her, that crazy melting part, wanted to lean her face into his, lift her fingers to his cheek and beg him to kiss her again.

"You were very tired last night," he said lowly. "You should have rested today. But I can see you didn't."

The blue scarf she'd been wearing this morning was gone and now her long hair fell in disheveled waves around her face. There was dust on her face and clothes, beads of sweat on her upper lip and dark shadows of fatigue under her eyes.

Her beauty stirred the man in him, but it was her weariness that touched something deep inside him. She was a soft, gentle woman. She shouldn't have to work like a man. But he supposed it was the choice she'd made for herself. Or had Tomas's philandering taken away any sort of choices she might have had?

"Rose, had your father taken out other mortgages on the Bar M?" he asked with sudden bluntness. "I'm talking about loans other than the one I made him."

Where was this coming from? Rose wondered. She'd thought he was going to say thank-you, goodbye, see you tomorrow, then let her be on her way.

Stifling a sigh, she switched off the engine and looked at him. "No. At least we don't know of any other loans. There were all sorts of loans at the bank where he'd purchased cattle and horses. But thank goodness, the livestock had been used as collateral. We sold all those to pay off the promissory notes."

"I know you probably think I'm prying," he said, "but there's a reason for my asking."

She didn't want to look at him when he was close to her like this. It made her remember when she'd believed in the love of a man and a woman, in marriage and all the things that came with living together. In short, looking into Harlan's face made her very, very vulnerable.

"What is it?" she asked.

"There is a way you and your sisters could get out of this mess. And I'd be perfectly comfortable with the idea."

"A way out? Of debt, you mean?" she asked guardedly.

He nodded. "You could sell the Bar M. Pay off your debt to me and have the awful burden of keeping it going lifted from your shoulders."

"Sell it? To you, I presume?"

He looked truly surprised by her assumption. "Good heavens, no! What makes you think I'd want to purchase the Bar M?"

Her gaze moved from him to a bug splatter on the windshield. "Well, you are a Texan and they like things big."

His deep laughter tugged her eyes back to his face. "Believe me, the Flying H is plenty big enough for this Texan."

"Maybe so. But you've got to admit you could use the water."

He lifted the battered straw hat from his head and combed his fingers through his hair. As Rose watched him she wondered what it would feel like to run her fingers through those dark, damp strands, to lock her hands at the back of his neck and draw his head down to hers.

"Rose? Did you hear me?"

She stared at him blankly, totally stunned at how far her thoughts had taken her. "Oh—I was thinking about—about something else. What were you saying?"

"I was saying it would be to my financial advantage to drill wells on my own place rather than purchase the Bar M for water."

"Yes. I suppose so," she said, hoping her cheeks didn't look as red as they felt. If he were to ever know the erotic images she had of him, it would be disastrous. "And I'm sorry if I sounded suspicious, but after everything that has happened I can't help but think the worst. I don't think I'll ever be able to trust…well, I guess I'm always going to have my guard up."

She didn't have to tell Harlan she was full of mistrust. He could see it all over her, hear it in her voice. He'd been aware of it the first time she'd come here to talk to him. Yet the more he thought about it, the more he decided that her suspicious nature didn't all stem from her father's sleazy behavior. This morning, she'd declared it had been years since she'd allowed a man near her. There had to be a reason for that. But would she ever open up enough to tell him? And why did he want to know? The more he learned about her, the harder he was liable to fall. He needed to remember that.

"Look Rose, I don't want the Bar M. I just want things to be better for you."

Did he really mean that? For once in her life, could Rose believe a man might consider her before himself? She tried to smile at him, but suddenly there was a lump in her throat.

"The Bar M is my home, Harlan. I'd never be happy without it."

Harlan had expected her to say something like that. She was that sort of woman. Loyal to her home and family. In fact, he would probably have been a little disappointed in her if she'd said anything else.

"I understand," he said gently, then stepped back from the door. "I'd better let you go now. Is Emily planning on helping you tomorrow?"

Nodding, Rose started the engine. "We're going to line ride tomorrow. So if you'd bring her horse with you in the morning, I'd appreciate it."

He lifted his hand in farewell. "I'll have them both there in the morning."

Rose gave him an awkward little wave, then quickly drove away. It wasn't until she was far away from the house that she was able to relax her grip on the steering wheel. But her hands immediately began to shake, forcing her to once again tighten her fingers on the laced leather.

The man hadn't so much as touched her, yet she felt as if she'd just spent a reckless hour in his arms. Her heart was racing, her face burned, and her hands shook like an alcoholic's.

Rose unconsciously pressed down harder on the gas. She had to get home and away from Harlan Hamilton.

"Harlan's daughter is such a sweet little thing," Kitty spoke up later that night as the family sat around the supper table. "I'm glad you've invited her to spend some time with us. She seems hungry for company."

Rose pushed a pile of stir-fried vegetables around on her plate. "She was very sullen the first time I met her."

"After spending time with her today, it's hard to picture Emily as sullen," Chloe said.

Rose didn't want to talk about Harlan or Emily. There were plenty of other happenings in the area they could discuss over supper. But her sister and aunt seemed taken with the subject of their neighbors to the east.

"I know. Harlan credits me with the change in her. He says she took a quick liking to me." She lifted her gaze from her plate to see Chloe and Kitty had both stopped eating and were staring at her as if she were about to break open some deep dark secret.

"That's not surprising. I don't know of anyone who doesn't like you, Rose," Kitty said.

Rose had always been too quiet by nature to be much of a socializer. But those people she did come in contact with from time to time, she treated with friendly respect. Yet as far as being someone's dearest friend, she wasn't. Other than her sisters, she'd never been able to let herself be that close to anyone.

"I don't know about that. But I think Emily was just waiting for someone to come along and befriend her. She lives a lonely life. Especially in the summer when school is out and it's only her and her father."

"Is Harlan good to her?" Chloe wanted to know. "Or is he one of those hard, demanding fathers?"

Harlan hard and demanding? Rose couldn't imagine it. She glanced across the kitchen at the twins, who had already eaten and were both now sound asleep on the floor of their playpen. The image of Harlan holding Adam so gently and lovingly floated through her mind.

"Quite the contrary. He's very easy with his daughter."

Chloe pondered this as she reached for her water glass. "Well, that's not surprising. She's a part of the wife he lost."

"He must have been crazy about the woman."

Kitty's remark turned Rose's attention back to the dinner table. "What makes you say that?"

With a negligible wave of her hand, Kitty rose from the table and went to pour herself a cup of coffee. "Because he's never remarried. As far as I know he hasn't had much in the way of girlfriends, either."

Rose frowned. "How could you know that? I didn't think you knew Harlan."

Coffee cup in hand, Kitty returned to her seat at the table. "I've spoken to him briefly a few times when he stopped by the ranch to see Tomas. But as for the girlfriends, I'm merely repeating rumors I've heard."

And in this case, rumor was right, Rose thought. The first night she'd met him, Harlan had implied he wasn't interested in attaching himself to a woman. Not even in a semipermanent way. But whether his single status was due to some overwhelming grief for his late wife, Rose couldn't say. Nor did she like the idea of Harlan clinging uselessly to a memory. He was too strong a man for that.

Dabbing her mouth with a napkin, Rose pushed her chair back from the table. The food on her plate had barely been touched, but her appetite was completely gone now.

"Well," she said to her aunt and sister. "The only thing we need to know about Harlan Hamilton is that we owe him money. Whether he wants a wife or a mother for Emily is his own business."

She left the kitchen with both women staring worriedly after her.

Later that night Justine called as Rose was helping Chloe give the twins a bath. Rose dried her hands and went into the study to pick up the phone.

"Hi, Rose. Sorry I called at a bad time."

"Don't worry, Chloe is managing all by herself. Although I'm not sure who's actually getting the bath, her or the twins."

Justine laughed. "Either way, I'm sure Chloe is enjoying every minute of it."

Yes, Chloe was utterly taken with her baby brother and sister. Rose often worried what it might do to her if Belinda suddenly showed up to claim the twins. One thing was for certain, her little sister would be totally heartbroken.

"How's everything over at the Pardee Ranch? Charlie and Roy doing okay?"

"Charlie has been happily helping his daddy dig holes in the yard. Roy wants to put up a fence around the house and plant rosebushes. For his beautiful wife, he says."

"Rosebushes?"

Justine laughed and Rose could easily tell it was the contented sound of a woman who knew she was loved. Justine and Roy had been married for more than two months now. But before that things had hardly been easy for the couple. Five years ago Justine had borne Roy's son, but at the time she'd believed he loved someone else more. So she'd left town and kept the baby's parentage a secret from him. Once Roy had discovered the truth about Charlie, he'd been furious. But in the end love had prevailed and both Justine and Roy now regretted letting pride and misunderstanding waste five years they could have spent together.

"Romantic huh?" Justine went on. "But I told him this isn't east Texas, it's the New Mexican desert. He still insists he can get them to grow and bloom."

"When Roy gets them all planted I'll come over and take a look. I haven't gotten to see Charlie enough lately."

"I'll hold you to that promise, sis. So how are things going over there?"

Rose bit back a sigh. She didn't want Justine to know just how weary she and Chloe were; it would only make their middle sister feel guilty for not being around to help. Justine's monetary contribution to the ranch each month was doing more than her fair share to hold the Bar M together.

"We're all fine. Has Roy made any progress tracing Belinda Waller?"

"That's mainly why I'm calling. He's tracked her to a cheap apartment in Albuquerque, but the police up there tell him she hasn't been seen around the place for the past several days. I think Roy is going to drive up there tomorrow to search the apartment. Even if Belinda isn't there, he might find something to tell him where she's headed or something about her plans. But I think it would be like hoping for snow in July to think she still might have any of the money that Daddy sent to her."

Rose grimaced. "It doesn't sound like she's living as if she has much money."

"No. I think we can safely write off those thousands."

Rose rubbed fingers across her furrowed brow. It sickened her to think that Harlan's hard-earned money had been lost, too. And she suddenly realized he had been victimized just as she and her family had been.

"When do you think Roy will be able to tell us what he finds in Albuquerque?"

"He's not planning on staying overnight, so I'll call you as soon as he gets back home."

Rose propped her thigh over the corner of the massive oak desk and closed her eyes. "Justine, I'm so worried about Chloe and the twins. She wants to be their mother so badly. What if Roy discovers Belinda wasn't the one who dumped them here? What if they were kidnapped from her, then left here? The woman would have every right to claim her own children!''

''I know, Rose. But Roy tells me that's a highly unlikely scenario. For one thing, Belinda was identified by Fred as the woman with the twins that day in Ruidoso. Second, why would a kidnapper leave the babies on the Bar M? A kidnapper certainly didn't know the twins were our siblings. Think logically, Rose. Belinda left the babies with Tomas and his daughters.''

Rose's eyes flew open. ''You mean the woman probably doesn't know Daddy is dead?''

''Roy thinks she might not. After all, who would have told her? If Daddy was driving down to Las Cruces to see her, all she knows is that his visits and his money have stopped.''

Rose let out a heavy sigh. ''I hope Roy is right.''

''He usually is. That's why he's such a good sheriff.''

Rose smiled. ''You wouldn't be a bit prejudiced?''

Justine chuckled. ''Not in the least. Just agreeing with ninety percent of Lincoln County voters,'' she said with glee, then her voice sobered. ''Darling Rose, don't worry. And don't let Chloe worry. Roy is going to find Belinda Waller and when he does, he'll make sure she pays for what she's done to our family. You've got to trust him.''

If there was one man on this earth Rose could trust, it would be her brother-in-law. ''You're right, Justine. And we'll try to think positively about this.''

''Well, I'd better let you go. Charlie is helping his dad load the dishwasher, so I'd better go take a peek. They've probably thrown in food scraps and all!''

''Okay. I'll talk to you tomorrow night.''

''Oh Rose, before you hang up, I wanted to ask about Harlan Hamilton.''

Every nerve in Rose's body tensed at the man's name. ''What about him?''

"I just wanted to know how things were going with him. Is he quibbling over the money?"

No, he was quibbling over her. The thought hit Rose so strongly she very nearly said the words aloud. Wouldn't that shock her sister? she thought wildly. "No. He's—contented to gain access to our water and pasture. So far."

Justine sighed with relief. "Good. I hope you can keep him that way."

Rose wasn't sure what it would take to keep a man like Harlan contented. Nor did she know why she'd been relegated to the task. But she did know one thing. She was going to have to get a firm hold on herself before she did something foolish. Like fall in love with the man.

"I hope so, too," she murmured huskily. "Good night, Justine."

The next morning, Rose was surprised to find Emily waiting outside by the corrals. Her Appaloosa was already saddled and tied to a nearby hitching post. Harlan or his truck and trailer were nowhere in sight.

"Good morning," she greeted Emily. "I didn't realize you were out here. I thought you would come to the house."

Smiling, Emily shook her head as she moved into step beside Rose. "Daddy was in a hurry this morning. He says he has lots of stuff to do today. And anyway, he says it isn't good to wear out your welcome."

"Oh. Well, neither of you have to worry about that around here," Rose said, while hating herself for being disappointed. All evening she'd thought about seeing Harlan again this morning, but he'd already come and gone without even saying hello. Instead of feeling relieved she was totally deflated.

The two of them walked on toward the stables. Pie and

the other working horses were kept at one end of the long barn, away from Chloe's racehorses.

While Rose brushed and saddled the sorrel, Emily stood near her shoulder, handing her blankets and tack and sporadically patting Pie's rump.

"Are we going to ride far today, Rose?"

"As far as we can before noon. Did you bring your lunch?"

"No," Emily said ruefully. "I forgot and left it in the refrigerator."

"Don't worry. I've already packed enough for the both of us."

Rose glanced at the teenager and saw a relieved look cross her face.

"Gee, Rose, you must have been an awfully nice teacher."

Rose smiled to herself as she adjusted the latigo. "Why do you say that?"

"Because you don't get mad about things and yell and threaten."

That didn't mean she didn't sometimes want to get angry, to yell at the top of her lungs and stomp her feet as Chloe sometimes did when she lost her temper. But Peter's assault all those years ago had not only frozen her desire for men, it had also made it hard for Rose to express much outward emotion. If she was hurt she did her best to hide it. If she was angry she tried her best to dampen it. Most of the time Rose lived inside herself and most of the time she was a very lonely woman.

Annoyed with her straying thoughts, Rose jerked both stirrups into place and reached for the reins. "Come on, honey. If you're ready, we'd better get started. We've got a lot of ground to cover."

The two of them rode west to a section of the ranch that hadn't been used much in the past few years. The pasture was a long distance from the main ranch house, making it a nuisance if an animal needed to be moved or doctored. Also, several miles of the land ran adjacent to an isolated county road. The perfect setup for cattle thieves. However, it had been more than a decade since cattle theft had taken place on the Bar M, so Rose wasn't really worried about that matter. She was more concerned about the condition of the fence.

For two hours she and Emily rode through sagebrush and scrubby piñon pine. They were almost to the outside boundary fence when Rose spotted the cattle. As the two of them neared the herd, the animals lifted their heads but didn't bolt from the patch of prickly pear.

"Do they look okay?" Emily asked.

"I think so. Let's take a closer look," she told the girl.

The morning sun had grown unmercifully hot. Rose pushed her hat to the back of her head and wiped her brow on her shirtsleeve before riding a few steps closer to the herd.

Surprisingly, despite the lack of grass and the searing heat, the cattle appeared to be in pretty good shape. But something didn't seem right. Rose squinted her eyes as she studied every animal in the group.

"The bull is gone!" she said with a sudden gasp.

Emily jerked around in the saddle. "Gone! Are you sure, Rose?"

Rose tried to swallow down the knot of fear forcing its way into her throat. The bull was a pureblood worth thousands of dollars and probably the best bull on the whole ranch. If he was dead, she didn't know if she or the ranch could bear the loss.

"I don't see him."

Emily looked worriedly from Rose to the herd of cattle. It was the first time she'd heard Rose raise her voice over anything.

"He's got to be here somewhere. He was here the other day when we moved the cattle," the teenager reasoned.

Rose nodded and tried to calm herself. The bull could have simply wandered off away from the herd. "Let's look around here and see if we can find him. I'll ride to the west. You go east. But don't get so far away that I can't find you," she told Emily.

Emily reined the Appaloosa away from Rose and took off at a short lope. "I'll find the bull for you," she yelled over her shoulder.

Twenty minutes later Rose still hadn't caught sight of the bull anywhere. She was about to turn around and go in search of Emily when behind her, she heard the girl shouting.

"Rose! Come and see what I've found!"

Rose galloped over to where Emily waited on a barren rise of land. "What is it? Did you find his carcass?"

"No! I haven't seen the bull. It's the fence. Someone has cut it down."

Rose stared blankly at the girl. Surely she hadn't heard right. "The fence is down?"

Emily nodded as she heaved to regain her breath. It was then Rose noticed the hot lathered condition of the Appaloosa. "You've galloped for a long distance."

Emily nodded again. "I was a long way from here when I found the fence. And then—well, I got scared! What if moonlighters did it? They might come back!"

"Show me the fence," Rose said grimly.

Thirty minutes later Rose squatted on her bootheels to examine the area around the cut fence. The six strands of barbed wire lay in useless curls on the ground.

"Emily, what kind of boots are you wearing? Do they have a track on the bottom?"

"No. They're slick leather soles. Besides, I didn't get off my horse. Why?"

Rose peered closer at the dim footprints in the loamy desert soil. "Because whoever was here has a small foot about your size."

"Do you think they got the bull?"

"I don't know. I hope not. But it looks like his tracks are here, too." Rose straightened to her full height, then carefully stepped through the tangled wire and out toward the county road. It didn't appear as though a stock trailer had parked on the side of the dirt road. Nor were there any scuff marks on the ground indicating where a large animal might have been loaded into any sort of vehicle.

"Why would someone cut your fence, Rose?" Emily asked once Rose had rejoined her. "Is there somebody around here who doesn't like you or your family?"

Rose couldn't imagine anyone. But after all that had happened here lately, she couldn't be sure about anything anymore. "Not that I can think of."

"Well, someone meant harm when they did this," Emily said with adultlike speculation. "We'd better get back fast and tell Daddy!"

Rose looked at the girl. "Tell your daddy? Why?"

Emily threw up her hands as if she couldn't believe Rose had to ask. "Because he'll know what to do. Because he'll help you, Rose."

Harlan? Help her? Yes, she supposed he would. He'd more or less intimated he'd help her with anything, if she'd only ask him. But did Rose want to ask? It would only draw him closer to her. She knew that as surely as she knew every hill and coolie on this ranch. Did she dare risk it? Did she need him that badly?

With one graceful sweep of motion, Rose was back in the saddle, reining Pie toward the Bar M.

"Let's go find Harlan," she said.

Chapter Seven

Back at the Bar M, Rose dialed Harlan's number and was lucky enough to catch him in the house eating lunch. She quickly relayed what she and Emily had found, then went on to ask him if he'd be willing to help her.

"I'll bring my horse and be right over, Rose. In the meantime, I want you to call your brother-in-law and tell him exactly what you told me."

In spite of the heat in the study, goose bumps covered Rose's skin. "Call Roy? You think the law needs to be involved?"

"That fence didn't cut itself, Rose. Someone is up to no good."

Of course Harlan was right. But the idea of someone deliberately stealing or harming Bar M cattle was so evil Rose didn't want to think it could actually be happening.

"All right. If you think I should, then I'll call," she promised him. "Emily and I will be waiting here at the ranch for you."

"Give me twenty minutes."

"We'll be down at the stables saddling fresh horses. And Harlan?"

"Yes?"

She gripped the receiver tighter and blinked as moisture filled her eyes. "Thank you."

"Rose," he said softly, "it's going to be all right. I promise."

She knew he was trying to comfort her, but at this moment Rose didn't know if anything would ever be all right again.

"I'll see you when you get here," she said in a voice not much more than a whisper.

Even though it was much farther to drive around to the back of the ranch, Harlan decided it would be better than riding the horses anymore than necessary in the afternoon heat.

On the way, Rose sat wedged between Harlan and Emily, who was hanging her head out the open window, scanning the passing landscape for any sign of the bull.

"Did you talk to your brother-in-law?" Harlan asked as they headed east down the county dirt road.

Rose didn't turn her head to look at him. She was already too aware of his closeness. His thigh was pressed along the side of hers and their shoulders rubbed with each little bump and sway of the truck. She was sweating and not just because of the heat.

"He's gone to Albuquerque today and won't be back until late this evening. He had a lead on the mother of the twins and thinks she might be living up there."

Rose could feel him glancing at her. "Are you anxious for him to find her? Or would you just as soon she disappear off the face of the earth?"

Rose thought about this for a moment. "I can't imagine facing the woman. If she was standing right in front of me

I don't know what I would say to her. Maybe I'd ask her why she wanted to hurt my father and the twins. And if she's done the things we think she has, then I believe she should have to suffer the consequences. But in any case, we must find her, Harlan. Otherwise, there will always be the threat that she might return to claim the twins."

"I can't imagine a judge returning the babies to her. Maybe after she served time, but even then I think the chances of that happening would be slight."

Rose certainly hoped he was right. "I told my sister Justine about the fence and the bull. She says Roy needs to see the crime scene. I told her I wasn't yet sure a crime had happened."

"Defacing property, endangering motorists and livestock. I'd call that a crime."

He sounded angry. At the moment Rose was more scared than anything.

"Aren't we almost there, Rose?" Emily asked as she ducked her head back inside the cab. "This land is starting to look familiar to me."

"I believe we'll find it right up the road on our left." Rose raised herself up in the seat for a better view out the window to Harlan's left. But after a quick glance at the Bar M rangeland, her gaze was drawn to his face. In spite of all her reluctance and misgivings, it suddenly dawned on her that this man gave her a strength and courage she didn't know she possessed.

The uncertainty in her gray eyes brought Harlan's hand to her knee. He could feel her quivering and wished his daughter wasn't riding in the pickup with them. He would have liked to pull to the side of the road and simply hold her in his arms until she quit shaking.

"Rose, it won't help to think the worst right now."

"Daddy's right, Rose. If the bull is gone for good it still won't be the end of the world," Emily spoke up. "Daddy says if you took everything away from a man, he'd still be rich if he had his health.''

Harlan smiled wryly. ''I didn't know my daughter remembered my philosophizing. I guess I'd better start paying closer attention to what I say.''

''Well,'' Emily went on, ''that's the truth. Once you lose things you can always buy them back later. But when someone you love dies—that's when you really lose.''

Rose didn't know any adolescents whose thinking worked like Emily's. But then losing her mother at such a young age had left a mark on her. It had also forced her to grow up in ways that most children never have to.

Her eyes moist, Rose turned in the seat and cupped her palms around Emily's face. ''You're right, honey. Thank you for reminding me.''

''You're welcome,'' she said with a big smile, then before Rose could guess her intentions, Emily leaned forward and pressed a kiss on her cheek.

Too choked to make any sort of response, Rose merely smiled and brushed the girl's bangs from her brow, then squared back around on the bench seat.

For the second time today Rose felt herself on the verge of crying and the lack of control over her emotions totally bewildered her. She was a woman who rarely cried over anything. Her father had always called her his strong, quiet girl. So what was happening to her? When Harlan was kind to her, tears burned her eyes. And now that Emily had kissed her she could hardly swallow down the lump in her throat. Were Harlan and his daughter making her soft? Or just melting her frozen heart?

''Rose, do most people around here know this land belongs to the Bar M?''

The three of them were standing a few feet away from the downed fence. A hot wind was blowing from the south-west and Rose's mouth already felt like cotton. If the bull had simply wandered through the fence, there was no way of knowing if he could reach water. In this heat, the animal couldn't survive long without it.

"I think so. Other than you and Emily most of the people who live in this immediate area have been here since before I was born. But that doesn't account for the people around Ruidoso."

"Is there any sort of sign along this stretch of the ranch, marking it as the Bar M?" Harlan asked, then glanced over his shoulder at Emily who was meandering over to the downed fence. "Don't get any closer," he warned her. "Sheriff Pardee will more than likely want to get a look at the footprints."

Rose waited until he turned back to her before she answered. "I don't know—wait, I'd almost forgotten there's a back entrance to the ranch, not far from here. Daddy had a pipe arch built over it. The name Bar M is etched in iron along with our Bar M brand. Anyone passing by on the road could easily read it. In fact, my sisters and I teased Daddy about making a big deal of the sign."

Beneath the low brim of his hat, Harlan scanned the horizon to the west. They had already passed that way in the truck and hadn't spotted any cattle.

He turned east and walked down the road, studying the ground for any sign of footprints or hoof marks. Rose and Emily followed a few short steps behind him.

"Look! Here's a few cattle tracks. It looks as though your fella headed this way."

Rose tried not to stem the hope rising up in her. "Then you don't think someone loaded him up and hauled him away?"

Harlan paused in the middle of the road. Rose stood beside him, her hands on her hips as her eyes continued to search every hill and dip for a sight of the lost animal.

"Strange as it may seem, I don't think so. I believe he found the hole in the fence and decided to go for a stroll."

Years ago when most of the land was more or less unsettled open range, it was harmless for cattle to go astray. A rancher merely took a handful of wranglers and rounded them up. But now that there were highways and county roads to be reckoned with, it was a serious matter. Huge lawsuits could result over car accidents involving livestock. Losing the bull would be bad enough, Rose thought, but a lawsuit would be the straw that broke the Bar M's back.

"Someone cut the fence purposely. What was their intention if it wasn't to steal the bull?" she wondered aloud.

"Meanness. Mischief. Spite. Could be a number of reasons," Harlan said with a shrug, then motioned for Emily to join them back at the truck. "Come on, let's ride this way for a mile or two and see if we can find him."

Nearly two hours later they found the bull in an arroyo a few yards off the road. He'd obviously gone there searching for water, but the drought had long ago dried up any little water holes to be found. The animal was gaunt with dehydration and Rose quickly said a prayer of thanks for finding him before it was too late.

Later that evening, after they had got the bull safely back home, Rose tried to express to Harlan just how grateful she was for his help.

"I should offer to pay you something," she said, as the two of them stood beside the corral watching the bull eat and drink to his content. "But I know it would only offend you. So I'll just say thanks and ask you to share supper with us. I don't know what Kitty's cooking tonight. But it's always good."

Funny that the issue of money had first brought Rose to him. Yet money was the very last thing he wanted from her now and it pleased him enormously to see that she was finally realizing that.

"Thank you, Rose, supper sounds very nice. But right now something needs to be done about the fence, or the rest of your cattle will find the cut and the whole herd will be out on the road. Do you have any portable panels?"

Rose nodded. "In the barn. I'll show you."

She turned to head toward the huge tin building to the right of them, but before she could take more than two steps, Harlan's hand was on her arm.

"No. Don't show me. Just tell me. I'll find them."

It was still broad daylight and the two of them were out in the open where anyone might see, yet to Rose they might as well have been standing in a darkened room. She could see nothing but him, feel nothing but the warm grasp of his fingers pressing into her flesh.

"But I—you'll have to have help loading them. And—"

He swiftly shook his head. "I can manage. I've done it for years. You go on to the house and rest."

Maybe she should, Rose mused. She didn't need to spend another hour or more alone with him. But she wanted to, and that was very nearly as dangerous as actually doing it.

"Just because I asked you to help with the bull doesn't mean I expect you to do more."

He frowned. "I know that. I'm doing it because I want to."

She wanted to ask him why. But something stopped her. She might not want to know his reasons for helping her. And he might not really want to tell her.

He nudged her toward the house. "Go on. I'll see you when I get back."

Nodding, she turned and started walking away from him. But all the way to the house, she could feel his eyes following her and it was all she could do not to turn and look back at him.

At the house, Rose took a quick shower, then after a moment of indecision, pulled on a long gauze skirt of purple roses and a matching tank top. If Kitty and Chloe thought she was trying to look feminine for Harlan she didn't care. She was a woman, after all. And she had enough pride not to want to look like a dirty cowhand all the time.

Kitty was grilling sirloin steaks for supper. While Emily played with the twins, Rose helped her aunt prepare a salad and a casserole of scalloped potatoes.

By the time Harlan returned from putting up the portable fence, it had grown dark but the temperature still hovered near ninety. His shirt was soaked with sweat and Rose immediately felt guilty for not insisting she go with him.

"Come on and follow me," she told him. "I'll show you where you can wash."

She took him through a large living room, then headed down a long hallway. As Harlan walked beside her, he had to struggle to keep from staring. A subtle pink color was on her cheeks and lips and her wavy chestnut hair was tied high atop her head with a wide purple ribbon. The faint scent of sweet honeysuckle swirled around her and the folds of her skirt swayed gently with the rhythm of her hips. He'd never seen this soft, womanly side of her before and the difference was very unsettling to his senses.

"Supper is ready, so we'll eat when you're finished here." She pushed open a door and flipped the light switch.

Harlan stepped past her and into a roomy bathroom with pink fixtures. "I won't be long," he promised.

She shut the door behind him, then started back to the kitchen. Halfway there, she happened to think he might appreciate a clean shirt. In her father's bedroom, she found a white cotton shirt folded in a pine chest. Her father had been a big man with broad shoulders and thick arms. She figured the shirt would fit Harlan perfectly.

Back at the bathroom door, she knocked lightly. "Harlan?"

The door swung open and Rose came close to gasping. Harlan was standing in front of the lavatory, stripped to the waist. Soap and water dripped from his face and trickled onto his chest. Like a dumbstruck teenager, Rose's eyes followed the rivulets disappearing into the black matt of hair swirling around his nipples and across his chest. His heavy work shirts had kept his skin hidden from the sun, making it much lighter than his face and forearms. He looked so hard, so male, so naked that for a moment she forgot why she was standing there.

"You wanted to tell me something?" He glanced at her as he wiped a washcloth against the back of his neck.

"I—uh, I thought—you might like a clean shirt." She stepped close enough to lay the shirt on the corner of the vanity.

Harlan's hand reached out and snaked around her wrist before she could step back into the hallway. Rose's heart beat wildly in her throat as she lifted questioning eyes to his face.

"Thank you, Rose," he said huskily. "That was thoughtful of you."

"You don't have to hold onto me just to say thank you," Rose said pointedly, but her voice was hushed and shaky, telling him exactly what his nearness was doing to her.

One corner of his lips cocked upward. "Have you ever thought I might simply *want* to hold onto you, Rose?"

"No! Harlan, this is…" she glanced desperately over her shoulder, then back at him. "We're in the bathroom, for heaven's sake!"

Before she could guess his intention, he reached behind her and pushed the door shut, cocooning them together in the room.

"Don't tell me you've never stood in the bathroom with a man," he said, his soft voice full of amusement.

Her mouth popped open. "I'm a single woman!"

She said it as though that automatically excluded her from having any sort of connection with a man. Her primness in this day and age both amazed him and endeared her to him.

"What does that mean?"

She gasped. "It means I'm not promiscuous!"

He chuckled softly as his hand slid up from her wrist all the way up to her bare shoulder. "Rose, honey, this is hardly making you a fast woman."

Her nostrils flared as color swept into her cheeks. "You like making fun of me."

His dark brows lifted. "I'm not making fun of you. I'm enjoying you." His hand crept upward until the tips of his fingers were playing with her hair. "You look very beautiful tonight, Rose."

Her knees were beginning to feel like jelly, and she was sure the two of them had breathed in every last bit of oxygen from the bathroom. "Washing off a little dirt hasn't changed my looks."

Smiling, he moved his fingers to the soft curve of her cheek. "You're right. You looked beautiful with the dirt, too."

Groaning, she stepped back. He instantly followed and circled his arms around her waist. Rose felt herself swaying and was forced to grab hold of his bare shoulders.

"Harlan, you...promised to be my friend," she whispered in protest.

He tugged her closer until she was pressed against his naked chest and long, denim-clad legs. "That's true. But I didn't promise not to touch you again. Why should I make a promise I know I can't keep?"

Her heart was pounding so hard she was certain he must

feel it shaking against him. "Because you know I don't want this. I..."

Her words ceased as his lips covered hers. In the back of her mind, Rose knew she should lever herself away from him. And fast! But she couldn't. Just like he said, she wanted this. Wanted him. It was shocking how much!

His hands framed her face, his thumbs locked beneath her chin. Rose's fingers dug into his shoulder and her lips parted. The tip of his tongue slipped between her teeth and delved deeper into the warmth of her mouth.

Rose shivered and clung as the erotic taste of him filled her senses and heated her body. She wasn't afraid of his strong arms and hands. She wasn't repulsed by the taste of his lips or the intimate invasion of his tongue. And the realization was both thrilling and terrifying.

"I think," he said, lifting his head and drawing in a long breath, "that you'd better get out of here and let me finish before they all begin to wonder where we are."

How did he expect her to simply walk out and face everyone now? Her legs were so wobbly she doubted she could make it down the hall. And she knew without looking in a mirror that her face was red, her lips swollen.

"You weren't worried about that a minute ago," she observed in a voice that sounded oddly hoarse, even to her own ears.

Smiling, he reached for a towel and hurriedly began to dry himself off. "I'm not really worried about it now."

With one hand gripping the edge of the vanity, she watched him slip his arms into the shirt, then shrug it over his shoulders.

"Was this your father's?"

"Yes. I thought it would fit you."

"It does."

For a man with big hands and fingers, he made fast, graceful work of the buttons. When he reached the bottom one, he undid the waistband of his jeans and lowered the zipper. Rose jerked her gaze off him and studied the pink and white tiles on the floor.

"There. I'm ready. Let's go eat."

She looked up to see he'd stuffed the shirttail into his jeans and was safely dressed again. She opened the door and stepped into the hallway with Harlan right behind her.

"Oh—uh, there you two are. Kitty sent me after you. Supper is getting cold."

Rose whirled around to see Chloe coming from the bedroom end of the house. Dear Lord, her sister hadn't been thinking she'd taken Harlan to her bedroom, had she? It was bad enough that she'd caught them like this.

"We were just—" Rose began.

"Rose was just showing me the bathroom fixtures."

Chloe looked suspiciously from her sister's red face to Harlan's sheepish smile.

"Really? You don't have a bathroom in your house, Mr. Hamilton?"

Rose frowned at her sister, but Harlan laughed with genuine amusement. "Call me Harlan, Miss Chloe. And yes, I uh—do have a bathroom. But I've been thinking about making some changes. With the fixtures, that is."

Chloe smiled at him and Rose knew she didn't believe a word of his story. "Well, I hope you were pleased with what Rose showed you."

The smile on his face turned into a ridiculous grin and Rose wanted to sink into the floor.

"Oh, believe me, she helped me make up my mind. I know exactly what I want now."

The slashing of the fence and the hunt for the bull was the major topic of conversation at the supper table. Rose managed to tell her part of the story and comment in all the right places. She even succeeded in eating a healthy portion of steak and potatoes, but beneath her outward calm, she was a wreck.

Harlan was attracted to her physically. That in itself was hard to imagine. Most of the men she'd tried to date after Peter had found Rose too cool and prim for their liking. And that hadn't really upset Rose all that much. She'd hated their sexual innuendos and clumsy attempts to tempt her into making love with them. So why was Harlan any different? What did he see in her that other men hadn't? And why did she melt like a pat of soft butter if he so much as looked at her?

In honor of their guests, Kitty served coffee and dessert out on the patio in the courtyard. The high desert air had finally cooled somewhat, making the night breeze pleasant.

While everyone ate and talked, Rose sat quietly in a cushioned lounge chair and tried to make her mind go blank. So much had happened in the past weeks and months she felt as if she were on a freight train that had lost its brakes and was on the verge of jumping the track. Her whole life seemed out of control and she didn't have a clue how to right it again.

"Rose, I'd like to talk to you. Can we go somewhere more private?"

Rose looked around to see that everyone had gone back into the house except for her and Harlan. And she hadn't even noticed!

"More private?" she asked, her voice close to squeaking. "We're alone out here."

"Yes, but...I don't want Emily, or anyone else, coming out and interrupting what I have to say."

She stood and wiped her suddenly damp palms down the folds of her skirt. "Are you sure you only want to talk?" she asked skeptically.

Her question put a crooked grin on his face. "Yes. Just talk."

She wasn't sure she believed him. The glint in his brown eyes gave her the impression he had everything but talking on his mind. Still, Rose wasn't about to run from him like a frightened little girl.

"There's a bench out front beneath the pines. We could go there," she suggested.

He stood. "Fine. Lead the way."

They walked slowly to the courtyard gate, then down the drive and away from the house. The night was clear and the moon high enough to shed plenty of light for them to walk without fear of stepping on a sidewinder. Harlan remained close by her side, his hand lightly touching the small of her back.

"You have a very nice family, Rose. I can see why it's so important for you to keep this ranch going."

"I'd do anything for my family," she said, then glanced up at his shadowed face. Now that the heat of the sun was just a memory, he'd left his felt hat back in the house. His dark hair curled rakishly across his forehead and down on the collar of the white shirt. *Looks to die for.* Chloe had certainly described Harlan to a T.

"Funny that you should say that."

"Why?"

He glanced down at her. "Because I..." He shook his head and motioned his hand toward the bench a few feet away. "Let's sit down first."

Her heart thudding heavily, she joined him on the slatted wooden bench. As soon as she grew still, he reached for her hand. Rose gave it to him and resisted the urge to close her eyes as the warmth of his fingers enveloped hers.

"I think you realize how fond Emily has grown of you," he began and Rose got the impression he wasn't quite sure what he wanted to say next.

"Yes, I'm fond of Emily, too. But you didn't need privacy to tell me that."

"Give me time, Rose. I'm trying to go into this gently."

Gently? The word put her on sudden alert. If he had some sort of unpleasant news to break to her, she didn't want him to beat around the bush about it. "Just spit it out, Harlan. Dear Lord, after all I've been through here lately, I don't need to be handled with kid gloves."

"This isn't something I want to blurt out."

A pent-up breath rushed out of her. "Have you changed your mind about the money Daddy borrowed from you?" Her brows shot up. "You think we should sell the place and pay you off. That's what you're trying to tell me, isn't it?"

He groaned with frustration. "Rose, you're jumping to conclusions. And I told you this morning that the money isn't an issue right now. I'm trying to tell you that I've been thinking and—" His fingers lifted from hers and began to make smooth little circles on the back of her hand. "I think there's a way you and I can help each other."

She studied her sandaled feet and tried to get her shaky nerves back under control. "Oh."

He didn't go on and Rose finally lifted her head and their eyes met in the silvery moonlight.

"How can we help each other?"

He took a deep breath. "We can get married."

Rose's heart ceased to beat as everything inside her went utterly still. "You...can't be serious!"

"I'm very serious."

Her mouth fell open, but she didn't care. He'd completely stunned her. There was no way she could hide it. "But you—you don't care anything about me. You barely know me!"

Harlan grimaced. "Love isn't the only reason people get married, Rose."

Humiliation poured through every inch of her, until her face burned with it.

"I didn't say anything about love," she said, her voice low and gritty. "But when two people get married they need to at least know each other and care about the other's welfare."

"We know each other," he countered.

An incredulous laugh slipped past her lips. "No—no, you don't know me at all, Harlan. If you did, you wouldn't dream of asking me to marry you."

He took her face between his hands. "I know all I need to know. Emily is crazy about you. She'd love for you to be her mother. I'd love for you to be her mother."

And that was supposed to be enough? Rose wondered wildly.

"Is that what this is all about, Harlan? That you simply want a mother for Emily? You told me the first night I came to talk to you that there wasn't a woman on this earth you'd ever want to marry. Now you're inviting me to be your wife. I'm sorry, but that sounds pretty flaky to me."

"Forget I ever said that."

"Why should I?"

He growled with frustration. "Because things are different now."

"How so?"

A scowl wrinkled his forehead. "I should have known you'd be cool and practical about this."

Rose was feeling anything but cool and practical. Her heart was beating at such a frantic pace, she was light-headed. Or was the idea of becoming Mrs. Harlan Hamilton doing that to her?

"That's me. Cool, sensible, boring Rose. I told you. You don't know me."

He made an impatient sound in his throat. "Rose, I admit that we haven't known each other very long. But I think we know enough. And..." He took hold of both her shoulders. "I know we would be good for each other."

How could she be good for him? She wasn't a whole woman. She could never make any man happy. Especially one like Harlan. "What...makes you think so?" she asked huskily.

"I need a mother for Emily and you need a man to help you keep this ranch going. It's as simple as that."

Her heart was suddenly breaking and she wasn't sure why. It shouldn't pain her to hear Harlan say he wanted to marry her for convenience. But in truth, it did more than pain her. What little feminine pride Peter had left her was now squashed by Harlan's calculated proposal. She was a woman who would never be truly loved by any man. He couldn't have made it plainer.

"I see," she said very slowly. She moistened her parched lips with the tip of her tongue. "So a mother for Emily is what you're really after."

In the past few moments her face had turned to stone and Harlan knew that he'd hurt her in some way, but he wasn't sure how.

"Rose," he said gently, his palms sliding up and down her upper arms. "Please don't think I'm being a heartless ass. But I...I'm not going to insult you by pretending to have fallen suddenly and madly in love with you. We both know that would be as ridiculous as if you told me you'd fallen in love with me at first sight."

Maybe she had, Rose thought. Maybe that's why she was feeling so raw and broken. Dear God, don't let it be so, she silently prayed. She couldn't bear to be hurt by another man. Not now. Not after everything else that had gone on in her life.

"I guess I should thank you for being so...up front with me."

She didn't look any too happy with him and Harlan knew if he was ever going to get her to agree to this marriage, he was going to have to appeal to the sensible side of her. She was that sort of woman.

"I realize this isn't how you…uh, expected a marriage proposal to be. I know women are generally romantic and—"

She stopped his words with eyes like granite. "Contrary to what you think, Harlan, I've been proposed to before. And in the conventional way."

His jaw dropped. The fact that some man had asked her to marry him didn't surprise Harlan. But the obvious bitterness on her face did.

"I wasn't implying that you hadn't." He shook his head with frustration. "Look, Rose, I don't know what happened with that proposal, but—"

"You don't want to know either," she cut in sharply.

So now he was getting to the crux of things, Harlan thought. Her daddy wasn't the one who'd put her off men. It was someone else. Someone whom she'd put her trust in, then had it badly broken. But now wasn't the time to ask her to delve into her past. He wasn't even sure he wanted to hear about it. The idea of a man hurting Rose in any way sickened him.

He clasped both her hands in his and squeezed them tightly. "Look, Rose, you've already told me you're not interested in romance. And after my wife died I…well, I don't ever want to love someone like that again. For a long time I didn't care whether I lived or not. And if it hadn't been for Emily I don't know that I would have made it."

"If that's the way you feel, I can't imagine you wanting to get married again."

A gentle smile curved his lips and seeing it brought tears to the back of Rose's eyes. If that smile was only borne out of love, she thought, she could happily give him anything. But it wasn't. He wasn't even trying to pretend he loved her.

"A marriage between us, Rose, would be different. We wouldn't have all the emotional ties that cause each other pain. We'd be good friends. And Emily would have a family again. So what do you say, Rose? Will you marry me?"

Chapter Eight

Harlan wanted her to be his wife! What was she going to do? What did she *want* to do?

Slipping her hands from his warm grasp, she left the bench and walked over to a nearby pine tree. The trunk was huge and she leaned against the rough bark, heedless of its sticky resin.

"Rose?"

She heard him coming up behind her. Quickly, she sucked in several breaths of cool night air.

His fingers touched the back of her neck and she wilted inside.

"I know this is very sudden for you," he murmured. "But please don't say no."

She swallowed as her throat grew tighter and tighter. "Just what sort of marriage would this be?"

"What do you mean?"

She glanced over her shoulder at him. He was such a strong, handsome man. A man made to love a woman. He didn't need her for a wife. He needed someone who could be not only a companion and friend, but also his lover. If he didn't realize that, she certainly did.

"I mean—" Oh, how could she do this? She turned to face him. "Are you expecting us...to have a sexual relationship?"

The kiss they'd shared in the bathroom had probably given her the idea he expected their marriage to be consummated in every sense of the word. And the notion was certainly a provocative one to Harlan. He figured making love to Rose would be far sweeter than he could possibly imagine. But he also knew she would probably run like a rabbit if he made sex an issue.

"Rose, I'm not going to stand here and tell you I'm not attracted to you. Hell, any man who didn't have one foot in the grave would be. But I know you're not ready for that sort of commitment to me. You might not ever be."

Incredulous, she asked, "And you could live with that?"

His thumb and forefinger gently closed around her chin. "I've lived for seven years without a woman in my bed. I can continue. Maybe after we're married awhile, you'll know more how you feel about that."

He was making it easy for her. Far too easy, she thought. "Where would we live? I have so much work to do here."

"I'd like for us to live in my house. As for your work here, we're already driving back and forth every day. Besides, I intend to take over most of your workload."

What would her sisters think? Would they be relieved that she finally wanted a man, or that one wanted her? Or would they think the stress she'd been under lately had finally made her slip off the beam?

Groaning, she turned away from him and Harlan was suddenly more afraid than he'd ever been in his life. He didn't know why, but having Rose be his wife had become everything to him.

"I don't know, Harlan. This is all so much to take in."

He curved his hands over her shoulders but resisted the urge to pull her back against him. "If it makes any difference, once we're married I'll dissolve the loan I made to your father."

Stunned, she whirled around to him. "Are you—"

He threw his hands up in a pleading gesture. "Now Rosie, before you start thinking I'm trying to buy you, just simmer down."

She closed her mouth and crossed her arms against her breast. She wanted to be furious with him, but just hearing him call her Rosie was like a sweet stroke of his hand. No one had ever called her Rosie before. Those who knew her considered her too staid and reserved for such a playful name.

"I'm sorry, Harlan, but that's what it sounds like to me. And I'll be honest with you, I think you'd be getting the poor end of the deal."

He grinned. "You let me be the judge of that. Besides, it would be pretty foolish to demand money from my own wife, wouldn't it?"

She thought about this for a moment. "I guess it would be rather strange."

"And it would be to my advantage to simply let the money stay invested in the Bar M, don't you agree?"

"You mean, if I prosper from it, then you stand to prosper?" she asked.

He nodded and his grin deepened. "So now that we've got that all reasoned out, are you going to say yes?"

Her shoulders sagged. She hadn't begun to reason things out in her mind. But apparently he had. "I...you've got to let me think about it, Harlan. I can't just give you an answer now. This minute."

"When can you?"

How long would it take her to know if she wanted to be this man's wife? she asked herself. Tomorrow? Next week?

Next year? Maybe she already knew the answer but was just afraid to tell him.

"Tomorrow evening. When I bring Emily back home." Her eyes widened as another thought struck her. "You haven't said anything about this to her, have you?"

"No. And I won't until I know how you feel about it."

Grateful, she nodded, then said, "We'd better go in now."

By mutual agreement they started walking back to the house. Along the way Harlan's arm slipped around her waist. It felt warm and right there and for once that was all that mattered to Rose.

The next afternoon after several hours of line riding, Rose and Emily returned to the ranch house and found Justine, Chloe and Kitty sitting out on the patio in the courtyard. Charlie and the twins were playing quietly in the shaded area of the sandpile.

Justine quickly extended her hand to Emily. "You must be Mr. Hamilton's daughter, Emily. I've already heard lots of good things about you."

Smiling shyly, Emily stepped forward and took Justine's hand. "Nice to meet you, ma'am."

Justine laughed. "Please don't call me ma'am. I'm not that old yet. Just call me Justine."

Rose glanced fondly over at the busy children. "Looks like Charlie is keeping the twins entertained."

Justine laughed and Chloe said, "We're not sure if it's Charlie who's keeping them happy or getting to dig their hands in the sand."

Kitty sat up in her lawn chair and quickly poured two glasses of lemonade, then handed them to Emily and Rose.

"Wait till you hear Justine's news!" Chloe said, her face wreathed in smiles.

"Don't tell me something good has finally happened,"

Rose said with disbelief. She walked over to a nearby lawn chair and took a seat.

"Well, Roy and I think it's good, at least," Justine said with a chuckle.

"Roy found Belinda Waller up in Albuquerque," Rose guessed.

Chloe rolled her eyes. "You think I'd be smiling about that?"

Rose stretched out her legs and crossed her boots at the ankles. She was exhausted. She'd been in the saddle for several hot hours this morning, but she'd spent the whole night wide awake, staring at the darkened walls of her bedroom trying to decide what to do about Harlan's proposal. She still didn't have an answer for herself or for him.

"I don't know whether you'd be smiling or not, but we all know finding Belinda Waller is something that has to be done."

"Well, this has nothing to do with any of that, thank goodness," Chloe replied.

"Amen to that," Kitty added. "It's about time this family had some happy news."

Happy? Rose wasn't sure she knew what that word meant anymore.

"Then I guess you're going to tell me that Roy found the idiot that cut our fence."

Justine shook her head. "He's working on it, Rose, but there really isn't much for him to go on. A few footprints and maybe some fingerprints on the metal post. But it's highly unlikely those will even be on file."

Rose's shoulders sagged at this news. Emily came to stand beside her lawn chair. "Me and Rose have a bad feeling about that fence," the teenager told the other Murdock women. "We think whoever did it might try to do something else."

Justine nodded grimly. "So does Roy."

The whole group went quiet after that until Chloe stood and refilled her glass with icy lemonade. "Let's not dwell on that right now. Tell them the good news, Justine," Chloe urged her sister.

Her beautiful face glowing, Justine looked at her older sister. "Roy and I are going to have another baby."

"Wow!" Emily exclaimed. "There's gonna be babies all over this place!"

Everyone laughed and Rose got up from her chair to go kiss her sister's cheek. "Congratulations, Justine. This is wonderful news."

"Thanks sis, I know it probably seems crazy wanting a child when everything around here is in such turmoil, but Roy and I have lost so much time together and Charlie is already five. We want him to have a sibling before he gets too much older."

"And he should have one," Rose agreed with a happy smile for her sister. "When are you due?"

"The end of March."

"And I guess Roy is walking on a cloud about it," Rose said.

Justine groaned and laughed. "I'm two months along and he's already trying to keep me off my feet."

"What about your nursing job at the clinic, Justine?" Kitty asked.

"It's only three days a week. Roy wants me to quit, but I told him I wanted to work at least until my eighth month. The exercise will be good for me. And Doctor Bellamy will always be nearby if I need him."

For the next few minutes talk centered around the coming baby. Eventually Rose noticed Emily had slipped away from the group of women and was sitting on the sand a few steps away from Charlie and the twins. The sad, forlorn look on her face had Rose quickly walking over to her.

"Emily, is something wrong?"

Her eyes firmly planted on the playing children, Emily shook her head. "No. I'm okay."

The girl sounded anything but okay, Rose decided. She looked as though she'd just lost her dearest friend.

Squatting down beside the teenager, Rose said, "Did I say something to hurt or upset you? If I did, I'm very sorry."

Emily's eyes flew to Rose's concerned face. "Oh, no, Rose. I'm not mad or anything like that. I just thought I'd come over here and watch the kids and rest."

Emily never mentioned the word rest and normally she would be playing with the children rather than watching them.

"Are you sure you're feeling okay?"

Emily's eyes dropped to her lap. "I'm fine," she said in a small little voice.

Rose remained quiet for a few moments, then decided to make a stab in the dark. "Did it upset you to hear my sister is going to have a baby?"

Lifting her head, Emily nodded ruefully. "I guess that's dumb, isn't it? I mean, I think it's great that she's gonna have a baby and Charlie is going to have a little brother or sister. It's wonderful for you all. But it—it makes me kinda sad, too."

Rose reached out and smoothed her hand over Emily's shining blond hair. "Because you wished it were you who was going to get the brother or sister. Is that it?"

Emily nodded again, then rubbed the backs of both hands against her eyes. "That sounds pretty selfish to you, doesn't it? And childish."

Tears stung Rose's throat. "No. It sounds pretty human to me." She didn't go on to tell Emily that she, too, was having some pretty selfish feelings of her own at the news of Justine's pregnancy. Not that she wasn't happy for her sister, she was. In fact, she was thrilled for her. Still, Rose couldn't help but wonder why it had never been her turn to have a husband and child of her very own.

You can have a husband and child of your own, a voice inside Rose whispered. Harlan wants you to be his wife. He wants you to be Emily's mother.

Maybe that didn't necessarily mean passionate love or a baby for her, but at least she would have a family of her own, Rose reasoned with herself. It was more than she'd ever expected. But would it be enough?

"I'm sorry for being sulky, Rose," Emily said. She got to her feet and brushed sand from the seat of her jeans. "I'm going to go over and tell your sister how happy I am for her."

Rose caught her by the forearm. "Emily, you're a sweet young lady. And you'll always be welcome to consider my family as your family, too. Don't ever forget that."

"Thanks, Rose," she said, then grinned. "Me and you, we're a team, aren't we?"

Rose slipped her arm around Emily's small shoulders. "Yes, we're a team."

The hammer glanced off the nailhead and squashed Harlan's forefinger against the two-by-four stud.

"Damn it," he muttered under his breath as he attempted to shake off the stinging pain.

If he'd had his mind on his business, the hammer would have hit its mark rather than him. But all day long Harlan had found it impossible to concentrate on anything but Rose.

She would be bringing Emily home in a matter of minutes and soon she would be giving him the answer to his proposal. A few weeks ago, even a few days ago, if someone had told him he would be asking a woman to marry him, he would have laughed in their face. Moreover,

if they'd told him how desperately eager he would be for
the woman to say yes, he would have called them insane.

And maybe he had gone a little mad, he argued with
himself. For seven years he and Emily had been on their
own. Initially, after Karen had died, it had been hard just
trying to cope with the grief. Then the sheer magnitude of
caring for a small child had been thrust squarely upon his
shoulders. Yet somehow they'd survived and grown together. So why did he want to bring Rose into the picture?
he asked himself.

Because Emily was growing into a young woman. She
needed a mother's touch. She needed female guidance
about things he couldn't possibly know about or understand. And life here on the ranch would be a little sweeter
with Rose around. It was as simple as that.

A few minutes later Harlan heard the sound of a vehicle.
He stepped out of the barn in time to see Rose parking her
truck at the side of the house beneath the shade of a
scrawny piñon. Emily jumped out and hurried into the
house, Rose climbed more slowly to the ground, then shading her eyes with one hand, looked toward the barn.

Harlan waved to her. She waved back and started walking to him. By the time she reached the barn, Harlan's heart
was pounding and his palms were slick with sweat. He
couldn't ever remember feeling like this.

"Hello," he greeted.

She gave him a shy, nervous smile. "I told Emily I had
to talk to you about a few things so she went on into the
house."

"How did things go today?"

She nodded. "Okay. We didn't find anything amiss with
the cattle or the fence. Roy has looked the scene over but
he's not very optimistic about finding the person who cut
the fence."

Harlan wasn't surprised to hear this. Short of having an

eyewitness who just happened to be driving by while the fence was being cut, there weren't many clues to go on.

"Well, at least nothing else happened."

She rubbed her hands along the sides of her skirt. She'd taken a shower and changed clothes before she'd left home. The pale yellow sundress she was wearing had skinny straps that exposed her shoulders. Normally it was a cool garment, but this evening she was already damp with perspiration.

"My sister Justine had some news for us," she said.

Harlan reached for her arm. "Let's go into the alleyway. The draft through the barn is cooler there."

They went inside the big tin building and Harlan motioned toward several bales of hay stacked near the door of the tack room. Rose took a seat on one of the alfalfa bales and waited for him to join her.

"What sort of news did she have? Something about your father's mistress?"

Mistress. Rose shuddered at the word. "No. It was personal. She and Roy are going to have another baby."

"Oh." He took a seat inches from her. "I guess everybody was happy to hear that news."

The barn was filled with the pungent smell of alfalfa, worn leather and horses. A few feet away, a cat lay sprawled fast asleep on an empty feed sack. Rose had always felt comfortable in these simple surroundings, but tonight she was anything but relaxed.

"Everybody was happy. Although the news did upset Emily just a bit."

Harlan couldn't have been more surprised. "Upset? I can't imagine it. Emily loves babies. You see how she is with the twins. And she doesn't even really know your sister."

Rose sighed. "Knowing Justine doesn't have anything to do with it," she told him, then looked at him squarely.

"Emily was saddened by the news, because it reminded her that she might never have a brother or sister. And she wants one desperately."

His jaw dropped. "Are you just saying this?"

Rose frowned at him. "I don't say things just to hear myself talk, Harlan."

He stared straight ahead as an array of emotions paraded across his face.

After a while Rose broke the silence. "You didn't know your daughter wanted a brother or sister?"

Swallowing, he turned his head and looked at her as though she'd just wounded him with a knifeblade. "No."

"Has she told you how much she wants a mother?"

He shook his head. "Obviously she's told you."

Rose could see he was hurt that his daughter had opened up to her rather than him. Maybe it was wrong of her to have told him any of this. But Emily was the reason he'd asked her to marry him in the first place. How could she not tell him?

"She doesn't think talking to you about it would do any good."

Harlan grimaced. "Well, at least I anticipated her need for a mother. Surely that counts for something."

"Of course it does. You're a good father, Harlan," Rose said gently. "I'm not telling you any of this to try and put you down."

His brows pulled together. "Why are you telling me?"

Nerves were knotting her stomach and she realized her hands were clenched so tightly together they were aching.

"Because—you wanted an answer from me about marrying you and I thought I had an answer until…" His eyes were delving into hers, robbing the words from her tongue. "Now I…"

His expression solemn, he edged closer to her. "Are you

saying you had decided to marry me, but now you're unsure?''

Nodding, she glanced away from him. He caught her chin and turned her face back to his. "Why? Tell me, Rose. We can't work this out until you do."

How could they ever work it out? she wondered miserably. He wanted a marriage of convenience. And she…just wanted to be loved.

"Harlan, surely it's obvious to you. Emily wants a sibling. She wants a *real* family. Not what you're planning."

"Emily needs a mother much more than she needs a sibling. Besides, you're still a very young woman, Rose. After a while you may decide you'd like to have a baby."

A baby with him! The very idea made Rose tremble. Their relationship could never enter into the bedroom. If it did, their marriage would be over. Even if she could get up enough nerve to let him make love to her, she knew he would find her a hopeless sexual partner. He'd be disgusted and disappointed with her. Maybe she could bear that sort of humiliation from some other man. But not Harlan.

"I—I'd never consider bringing a child into this world unless it was conceived out of love. We're…nothing more than friends."

Friends. Somehow that word didn't describe the way he felt about Rose. He wanted to protect her, help her. He wanted to see her happy. But most of all he simply wanted to be with her. Did she not even feel that much for him?

"I can understand that you'd need an emotional commitment from a man before you could have his child. But you're not thinking logically, Rose. I'm not going to go out and marry some other woman simply because Emily wants a brother or sister. That would be worse for her than not having one. If I don't marry you, I'm not going to marry anyone."

Put like that, what could she say? "I don't know, Harlan.

Today, when I saw her sad little face, I couldn't help but think it would be a big mistake to marry you." She squared her knees around so that she was facing him head on. "You need a woman who you...could really love and who loves you."

Wry bitterness twisted his features. "I've already told you that's the last thing I need. You know how I feel about this, Rose. It's been seven years since Karen died. In that time I haven't gone looking for romance. And if you turn me down I still won't go looking for it."

In other words he wasn't going to change for Rose or any woman. Marrying her for convenience was as far as he was prepared to go. Even for Emily's sake.

Rising to her feet, Rose walked to the opposite end of the alleyway. Leaning against the open door frame, she watched the approaching twilight fall across the sage-covered hills.

Years ago when she'd first grown old enough to think about her future it had all seemed so simple. She'd wanted to have a marriage and family just like her parents had. At the time she hadn't thought those things were too much to expect or hope for.

Now it all made her feel very foolish and even bitter. Her parents' marriage hadn't been the true, loving relationship she'd once believed. Maybe she was naive to even think such a thing existed.

She heard his footsteps behind her, but still she flinched when his hands curved over the top of her shoulders.

"What are you thinking, Rose? Have I hurt you?"

"No." She'd been hurt long before Harlan had stepped into her life.

"But you're worried that I might."

He said it as a statement, not a question. As though he could see the fear in her heart.

"Whatever you're thinking, Rose, I want you to know I'm not a hard man. I could never be mean to you."

Slowly, she turned to face him. "I'm not afraid of that," she murmured.

His eyes drank in her pale skin, her luminous gray eyes and soft rosy lips. Shadows were haunting her face and Harlan wondered if she was thinking back to that other proposal she'd once gotten. "You're afraid of something?"

Rose was desperately afraid of falling in love with him. A part of her was terrified that she already had. "Marriage of any sort is a big step to take."

He smiled gently. "We'll take the step together."

The warm look on his face, the tender promise in his voice was Rose's undoing. She was hopelessly charmed by him. The idea of living with him for the rest of her life was scary, but it was also too tempting to resist.

Placing her palms against his chest, she said, "Then my answer is yes. I'll marry you, Harlan."

Once it dawned on his brain that she hadn't turned him down, he began to breathe again. Plucking one of her hands from his chest, he drew the back of it to his lips.

"You've made me very happy, Rose."

But in a few days or weeks from now, would she still be making him happy? It was too late for Rose to ask herself that question. She'd promised to be his wife. And Rose never broke a promise, no matter how painful it might become.

"You're going to do what!"

Pushing a weary hand through her tousled hair, Rose looked across the breakfast table at Chloe. The announcement that she was going to marry Harlan had completely shocked her younger sister. And rightly so, Rose thought. Her whole family had decided she was going to live the rest of her life as a spinster. Instead, she was going to marry one of the most eligible hunks in Lincoln County. It was still difficult for her to believe.

"You heard me, Chloe. I'm going to marry Harlan. Friday, to be exact. Do you think we can get some sort of small wedding planned by then?"

Kitty struggled to keep a mouthful of coffee from spewing across the table. "Friday! Rose, have you lost your mind? You're just now getting to know this man!"

Chloe tossed down her fork. "What has he done to you?" she demanded.

Color flamed in Rose's cheeks. "What do you mean? He hasn't done anything to me."

"Well," Chloe huffed, "he's done something. You're not thinking straight."

Thank God, she and Harlan had decided it would be better all around if they pretended to her family and Emily that they were getting married because they were in love. It would be mortifying to have to admit to her sisters and aunt that Harlan only wanted her because Emily needed a mother.

"I know what I'm doing, Chloe," she said flatly, then picked up her fork and whacked off a bite of pancake.

"Oh, you do," Chloe said dryly. "Well, what happened to the Rose who hates men, who vowed she'd never get married?"

She kept her eyes on her food. "A woman has the prerogative to change her mind. Besides, I never hated men. I've just kept my distance from them. Until now."

Groaning, Chloe looked helplessly at Kitty. Her face wrinkled with concern, the older woman turned to Rose.

"Honey, it isn't like you to be impulsive. Does this have…anything to do with the money we owe Harlan?"

Years of pent-up emotions propelled Rose to her feet. "You know, a congratulations, or we hope you'll be happy, Rose, would have been nice. But I guess you two just can't accept the fact that a man could want me for myself. You have to turn this into something cold and calculating."

Choking on a sob, she turned and rushed out of the room.

Moments later, Chloe knocked on the open door of Rose's bedroom. "May I come in?"

Without looking at her sister, Rose walked over to a chest of drawers and pulled out clean lingerie. "You might as well. You're already half in anyway."

Tossing the scraps of cotton onto the bed, Rose crossed the room to a walk-in closet and pulled out a pair of jeans. Chloe stared helplessly after her.

"I'm sorry, Rose, if Aunt Kitty and I sounded less than enthusiastic—"

Rose whirled on her. "Look, Chloe, you or Aunt Kitty don't have to pretend to be happy for me."

Chloe threw up her hands as she stepped further into the room. "It's not like you to be angry and defensive like this, Rose."

Rose closed her eyes and swallowed. "It's not everyday that a woman announces to her family that she's getting married. It would have been nice to have gotten a little love and support from you."

"Oh, Rose," Chloe said with a groan, "you know we all love you. That's why we want you to be sure about this. You've got to admit this is all rather sudden. And you haven't even hinted that you and Harlan—well, that there was anything between you. I mean, I know you two weren't looking at bathroom fixtures the other night, but I didn't think you were talking marriage!"

Rose knew she was behaving badly. But her emotions were so worn and raw that it was a struggle just to hold herself together. Her eyes on the floor, she said, "It happened quickly. And maybe it seems strange to you. But…Harlan cares about me. So much so that he's going to dissolve the promissory note our father signed."

Chloe gasped, then swung her head back and forth. "Rose, I don't know what to say! You're not...marrying him just because of the money, are you? Because you want to save the ranch? If that's the case, I won't let you sacrifice yourself."

Rose's head whipped up. "It's true I'd do most anything to save this ranch. It's the only home we've ever had. But I could never do such a thing to anyone. Much less Harlan."

Hearing the wobble in Rose's voice, Chloe crossed the room and put her arm around her sister's shoulders. "You sound like you really love this guy," she said with awe.

As soon as Chloe spoke, all the jumbled confusion inside Rose seemed to fall into place. She knew there was no more pretending, hoping, dreading. It was all settled now. Her heart had already decided it was going to love Harlan Hamilton whether she wanted it to or not.

"I do love him, Chloe," she whispered brokenly. "After Peter, I didn't think it would ever happen. I didn't want it to happen." Her eyes blurred with tears, she tried to smile at Chloe. "But Harlan is...different."

Relief suddenly filled Chloe's face. "If you love this guy that's good enough for me," she said, then smiled wickedly. "Now what do you want to wear? Are we going to have the wedding at our church? What about your bouquet? And a cake?"

Laughing with excitement, Rose reached for her jeans. "I don't know! You're going too fast! And right now there're chores waiting on us."

Chloe plucked the jeans from Rose's hands and tossed them over her shoulder. "We're going to forget about the chores for a while. Let's go tell Aunt Kitty we have a wedding to plan!"

Chapter Nine

The following Friday afternoon Rose and Harlan were married in the same small country church she'd been christened in. Chloe acted as her maid of honor while Justine and Emily were bridesmaids. Roy gave her away, and Harlan's best man was an old friend from east Texas, who flew in especially for the ceremony.

Rose wore an ivory, ankle-length princess-cut dress. Pearl combs held her chestnut curls atop her head while a pearl choker and drop earrings framed her face.

The church was packed with friends and well-wishers, but now that the ceremony and short reception were over, Rose couldn't recall half of the people who'd approached her with congratulations.

Since it was a small wedding, Rose had forgone the tradition of tossing her bouquet. The pale pink roses now lay on her lap as Harlan drove the two of them toward Ruidoso.

"There really wasn't any point in us going away for the weekend," Rose said as the pickup wound through the desert mountains. "Emily is going to be staying with Kitty and Chloe. It's not like we're newlyweds going on a romantic honeymoon or anything.''

Looking across the seat, he gave her a wry smile. "That's funny, I feel like a newlywed."

Her cheeks suddenly matched the color of the roses she was holding. "You know what I mean."

He sighed. She looked so elegant and beautiful, so different from the cowgirl who punched cattle in the dust and heat and rode her beloved Pie for miles over Bar M range.

"Have I told you how lovely you look, Rose?"

He hadn't. But he'd kissed her enough this afternoon to make up for it. She was still wondering if his display of affection had been for the benefit of family and friends or simply because the wedding ceremony had made him feel closer to her somehow. Whatever the reason, Rose had to keep reminding herself that the man didn't love her. He might look at her as though he did, but that was just his kindness showing.

"Thank you, Harlan. You look very nice yourself." Actually, nice wasn't the word for it. Wickedly handsome was closer to it. He was wearing a dark suit and matching tie. His hair had been trimmed to a more respectable length and the day-old growth of beard that was normally on his face had been scraped away.

If she'd been a real newlywed, she would be thanking him for his smoothly shaven face. As it was, there wasn't any need. She wouldn't ever be in danger of getting whisker burn on any part of her anatomy.

"I hope for the next two days you can forget about your ranch and mine," he said after a few more miles had passed. "You may not be thinking of this weekend as a honeymoon, but it is. At least, it's a honeymoon away from your work. You need to relax and enjoy this time."

How could she relax when just sitting here next to him was turning her insides to hot mush? How could she go on being the cool, practical Rose he expected her to be? What if she lost control and begged him to make love to her? It would be the death of their one-day marriage!

"I'll try."

He grimaced. "You sound like I'm taking you to the gallows instead of a nice, quiet motel."

She sighed. "It's just that…I'm more comfortable—"

"With Pie than you are with me," he finished before she could.

She opened her mouth to protest, then seeing the twinkle in his eye and dimple in his cheek, she realized he was teasing. Her coiled nerves relaxed a little.

She smiled at him. "Harlan, I've known Pie much longer than I have you. And he's always happy to let me be the boss."

With a soft little chuckle, Harlan reached across the seat for her hand. "Well, for the next two days, I'll be happy to let you be the boss, Rose."

Her husband was asleep. And so should she be. But Rose knew that sleep would evade her for several more hours.

Harlan had been thoughtful enough to reserve a room with two double beds. Rose had lain in hers for a while but after more than an hour of tossing and turning, she'd given up and come out on the private little balcony overlooking a long oval swimming pool.

The night was still warm and though the pool was empty of guests, the muted sounds of nearby traffic reminded her she was only a short distance from a nearby restaurant and lounge where people were eating, dancing, laughing and generally enjoying themselves.

During dinner, Harlan had tried his best to coax Rose onto the dance floor, but she'd remained frozen to her seat. It wasn't that she had two left feet. Rose knew how to dance and was fairly graceful at it. But she knew what being in Harlan's arms would do to her and she couldn't stand the temptation.

"What are you doing out here?"

At the sound of his voice, Rose glanced back over her shoulder. Harlan was standing in the doorway. A pair of white boxer shorts was the only thing covering his tall, muscular body.

Her heart hammered wildly as her gaze scaled up his legs, across his flat abdomen, then moved on to his broad, thick chest and finally stopped on his brown eyes.

"I—I'm just taking in the night."

He walked over to her and suddenly Rose was more aware of her skimpy attire than his. Chloe and Justine had given her a beautiful but filmy negligee for a wedding gift. The pale green chiffon did little more than keep her from being naked. If she'd had any sense she would have packed her cotton pajamas while her sisters hadn't been looking.

"You couldn't sleep?"

She shook her head.

"Neither could I," he admitted.

Careful to keep her arms folded across her breasts, she turned to him. "I thought you went to sleep a long time ago."

One corner of his mouth turned up wryly as his gaze dropped to her lips, then the bare skin exposed above her breasts.

"Just playing possum so I wouldn't disturb you."

He'd have to be gone from this state, from her very mind, before he wouldn't disturb her, she thought.

"You don't have to worry about being quiet for me. I often have trouble sleeping. I guess worries do that to a person."

Harlan couldn't help himself. He touched her hair where it lay against her bare shoulder. Immediately he heard her breathing quicken.

"You're not worried now, are you?"

She was. But she would never tell him. Her eyes dropped to his chest. "I was…just thinking about my family and Emily."

His fingers moved to her shoulder. Her skin was warm, pearly white and as soft as the petal of a rose. He knew the rest of her would be just the same, but he was trying not to think about that.

"You have a daughter now. How does that make you feel?"

"Very happy." And it did. For years now she'd resigned herself to the idea that she would never be a wife, much less a mother. Now she was both. Maybe not in the truest sense of the word. But Emily loved and needed her. And that meant a great deal to Rose.

"And what about me? You don't regret having me for a husband, do you?"

His calloused fingers sent shafts of heat radiating through her shoulder. She told herself she wished he would step back from her so that she could breathe and think. Yet what she really wanted was for him to crush her in his arms. To kiss her and touch her and tell her how much he loved her, how he would always love her.

"No, I don't regret marrying you. Do you regret having me for a wife?"

How could he, when just looking at her like this melted his heart?

"No," he murmured. "I'll never be sorry I married you."

Rose's heart swelled with emotion. It wasn't an *I love you,* but it was infinitely sweet to her just the same.

"You might be. Someday."

Her voice dropped to a raspy whisper on the last word and Harlan suspected she was very close to tears. Wanting to comfort and reassure her, he pulled her into the circle of his arms.

"Rose," he whispered. "I don't know why you would think such a thing."

She trembled as she felt her breasts press against his hard chest. "I'm not what most men expect of a woman."

His hand slid beneath her hair, then cupped the back of her neck and drew her closer. "No. You're more."

She groaned and buried her face in the side of his neck. "You...don't know. Oh, Harlan, I feel like I've betrayed you. I've cheated you—"

"What are you talking about?" he asked with wry humor. "You couldn't betray anyone even if you tried."

Suddenly tears were brimming over her lashes and spilling onto her cheeks. Horrified at their appearance, she lifted her head and dashed them away with the back of her hand.

"I'm a frigid woman, Harlan. I can't make love to a man." Squeezing her eyes tightly shut, she shook her head. "I should have told you all of this before we were married. But I was so ashamed. You see, I...I've never made love to a man before."

A part of Harlan was stunned by her admission and yet he'd somehow intuitively felt her innocence when he'd kissed her. Still, she wasn't a frigid woman. Maybe she thought so. But he knew better.

"Rose," he said softly. "Being a virgin isn't anything to be ashamed of."

She reared her head back far enough to look at him. "You don't understand, Harlan. If you decided you wanted me...for us to have a child, I couldn't..."

As her words trailed away it struck Harlan exactly how much this whole thing was tearing her apart. And then suddenly he began to see everything about her more clearly. *I don't make social calls on men. I haven't let a man get near me in years. I won't have a sexual relationship with you, Harlan.*

"Rose, what makes you think you're frigid?"

She drew in a long breath. "I just know. That's all."

His hand slid up the side of her neck until it was cupping her jaw. "Are you telling me that whenever I kiss you, you don't feel anything at all?"

"No! Yes! I mean—" Shivering at his touch, she paused and tried to draw a calming breath. "Harlan, don't ask me these things."

"Why?"

She groaned. "Because there's no use. If you want an annulment I won't be angry or hold it against you."

His arm came around her waist and tugged her closer. As Rose practically fell against him, she could feel his bare leg slipping between hers, the bulge of his manhood pressed against her hips.

"I'd rather hold you against me," he whispered.

Like a block of ice in the afternoon sun, Rose began to thaw. Her hands crawled up his chest and anchored themselves over the tops of his shoulders.

"You don't think I'm a cold woman?"

Cold? She was searing him like a hot brand, making him forget their plans to keep this marriage a platonic one.

"Do I have to answer that with words?"

Rose didn't know what had come over her. She'd never planned to tell Harlan any of this. But there was something about him that pulled at her, exposed her in a way that she couldn't understand.

"Harlan, you said...you didn't want me."

"I don't recall saying anything like that. If I did, I was temporarily insane," he countered.

His hands splayed around her waist, then slid to her back and up to her shoulder blades. Heat began to pulse through

Rose, filling places deep inside her that she hadn't known she possessed.

"It wouldn't be good for us to…make love tonight." Tomorrow or anytime, Rose thought wildly.

"I can't think of anything that would be more good," he murmured against the crown of her head.

Rose's knees were growing weaker and weaker, making her cling tighter and tighter to his shoulders.

"It would only make problems for us. We married for practical reasons."

Maybe they had, Harlan thought, but it seemed less and less like that now.

"You don't want us to be together…physically?"

Rose suddenly felt as if she were on a giant pendulum swinging to him and away from him. Should she end the ride in his arms or as far away from him as she could get?

"No. I mean…uh…maybe I'm—" Too torn to say more, Rose pulled out of his hold and hurried back inside the room.

Sitting on the edge of the bed, she covered her face with trembling hands. A wedding night wasn't supposed to be this way, she thought miserably.

"Rose?"

Her name came out softly, gently. She dropped her hands and looked up to see him standing over her. The raw intimacy on his face terrified her.

"Harlan, it's not a matter of wanting. It's—"

"Tell me." He eased down beside her and reached for both her hands. "What did he do to you?"

"He? How did you know…" She shook her head. "Who are you talking about?"

His thumbs caressed her knuckles. "The man who hurt you. The man who asked you to marry him. The conventional way."

Rose twisted her head away from him. "I don't want to talk about him. He isn't worth it."

"No. He isn't worth coming between us."

Harlan was right. Still, she hadn't told anyone about Peter. Except her family. But Harlan was her family now.

"I—was very young. In my second year of college at Eastern New Mexico State," she began. "Peter was a medical student there. And I...thought I was in love with him."

"You *thought?*"

Rose shrugged. "I'm not sure if I knew what love was back then. Does anyone, when they're nineteen years old?"

"Did you become engaged to this man?"

Rose nodded. "But as soon as Peter slipped a ring on my finger he...became possessive and demanding. He thought I should be ready and willing to jump into bed with him." She lifted her eyes to his. "I wasn't ready for that. Emotionally or physically. I had been raised to believe that sex was something that should happen within the sanctity of marriage. I guess that sounds laughable to you. Especially now, after what my father did. But at the time it was very important to me."

"Rose, a person's moral values are never anything to laugh about. If this man had loved you, he would have respected them."

"I finally realized that. And realized, too, that Peter wasn't really thinking of me in terms of his future wife. He simply wanted a sex partner while he attended college. So I...gave him back his ring and told him it was over." Her gaze dropped to their entwined hands. "He took it badly and accused me of stringing him along, then began yelling all sorts of vile, filthy things at me. He said I was nothing but a tease and that he wasn't about to let me cheat him out of what I owed him."

Harlan sighed with regret. "Oh, Rose, I hope you didn't believe him."

Unable to look at him, she shook her head. "By then it didn't matter what he was saying. It was what he did to me that…" Her throat closed on the words, forcing her to stop and swallow. "Well, I ended up having to fight for my life to get away from him."

Harlan's fingers tightened on hers. "Dear God, he didn't rape you? Did he?"

"No. Fortunately I wasn't fragile or petite and was in good shape from working on the ranch. I was strong enough to fight him off and get away. But I didn't escape unscathed. Both my eyes were blackened, my lips were split in several places, two ribs were cracked and the rest of my body covered with bruises and scratches."

Completely stunned, Harlan stared at her bent head. Of course he knew things like this happened. But not to Rose. She was such a loving, gentle woman. He couldn't comprehend a man laying an angry hand on her. He couldn't picture her beautiful white skin marred with ugly bruises, her luscious lips split and bleeding. It was too horrific to imagine.

"Rose. Oh, Rose," he whispered, stricken. "What you must have gone through."

"Before Peter, I was a sensitive young woman who could hardly bring herself to swat a fly. But afterward…I tell you, Harlan, I wanted to kill him. Literally. That's what his attack did to me. Then later…when I tried to date other men I simply froze whenever they touched me. And I guess I've stayed frozen…until now…until you."

Of all the things she'd said to him, this was like an arrow flung straight into his heart. She'd been hurt and betrayed by a man in the worst kind of way and yet she'd trusted him enough to marry him. The very idea swelled his chest with tender emotion.

Drawing her head against his shoulder, he stroked her hair and back. "My sweet wife," he murmured near her ear. "You should have told me before. You should have known I would understand." He tilted her face up to his. "You're not worried...you don't think I could ever hurt you like that, do you?"

Rose slowly shook her head. She knew he would never harm her physically. But what about her heart? He could break it without even trying.

"I wouldn't be here in your arms, if I did," she whispered.

It dawned on Harlan that the trembling in her body had quieted. Her hands were spread boldly upon his chest and her moist, parted lips were only inches away.

Leaning forward, he brushed his lips against hers. "We're husband and wife now. We have every right to make love. If we want to."

Everything around her, all the doubts and worries in her mind faded to insignificance as he planted warm little kisses on her cheeks, her throat, her chin.

"I don't want you to be...disappointed," she finished on a sigh.

Groaning, he pulled her up against him and covered her lips with his. The sweet bite of wild honey was on her lips, tempting him to search every curve and contour. But tasting her lips wasn't nearly enough to quench the need building inside him.

Thrusting his tongue between her teeth, he rubbed the tip of it against the ribbed roof of her mouth, then slowly glided it along the sharp edges of her teeth.

Rose's hands crept to his neck and clung tightly. Blood was pounding in her ears and rushing heat to every fiber of her body. His kiss was sucking her into a whirling vortex, urging her to follow him down a hot, erotic pathway.

By the time Harlan finally lifted his head, they were both

gasping for breath. "You couldn't disappoint me. Not like this," he whispered, brushing the back of his knuckles beneath her chin, along her jawline and down the side of her neck.

Rose's gray eyes pleaded with him. "You don't understand what I've been telling you, Harlan. I'm not a normal woman."

He made a mocking sound in his throat, then tilting his head, he nuzzled a spot beneath her earlobe. "You feel very normal to me."

"I'm afraid—"

Before she could finish, he quickly framed her face with both his hands and looked into her eyes. "You're not afraid of me. You told me so. And that's all that matters, Rose. This wanting between us is all that matters."

Once more he lowered his mouth to hers. With a groan of surrender, Rose slipped her arms around his neck and pressed her body into his. Her simple invitation was enough to make Harlan forget all about his plans to keep his feelings, his needs separate from his new wife.

He wanted her more than he could ever remember wanting anything in his life. It was too late to ponder. Too late to turn away from her.

Slowly, they sank sideways onto the mattress. Rose couldn't resist him as he pushed the negligee off her shoulders and down her arms. Once it was out of the way, he propped himself on one elbow and enjoyed the picture she made in her see-through gown.

"You're so beautiful, Rose. So very beautiful."

His palm settled against her flat belly, then slid slowly upward, stealing Rose's breath as it went. When his forefinger traced the edge of her nipple she closed her eyes and bit down on her lip.

She didn't know anything could feel like this. She'd

never dreamed *he* would feel like this. Every fiber in her body wanted him, needed him, burned for him.

His head bent and his mouth covered the tip of her breast. Fire shot straight to the core of her and she reached for him, pressed her body against his as love poured into her heart.

"I want you to make love to me, Harlan," she whispered with awed wonder. "I'm not afraid anymore."

Lifting his head, he smiled at her softly, knowingly. "I won't hurt you, Rose. Ever."

He sealed the promise with a kiss that grew deeper and deeper until they both began to shake with need. Then everything turned urgent as their hands and lips reached and strained for each other. Rose wound her legs around his and invited him to enter her. When he did, she was sure the world had stopped and heaven had moved in to stay.

Chapter Ten

Rose was in love with him. It wasn't merely a conceited notion on Harlan's part. Each time she touched him, he felt it. When she smiled at him, he saw it on her face. Every time she kissed him, he could taste it on her lips. And she kissed him often these days.

Since their wedding night two weeks ago, she'd definitely thawed and Harlan was suffering the consequences. Not that having a woman like Rose in his bed was a hardship. Making love to her was the closest thing to ecstasy he'd ever felt. And that was the problem. Every time he made love to Rose, he lost a little bit more of himself to her.

He'd once read somewhere that a woman made love with her heart while a man only involved his body. Harlan didn't know where that idiotic research had come from. It certainly wasn't working that way for him. And if he didn't put a stop to it, he was soon going to be head over heels in love with his wife.

Harlan couldn't let that happen. He'd never planned to

be that connected to her. He didn't want her to become so much a part of him that he needed her more than his own breath. What if he lost her? What if he woke one morning and had to face the fact that she was dying, leaving him the same way Karen had left him? He couldn't survive. Not this time. Not with Rose.

He looked up from the saddle he was oiling to see Rose pulling the pickup to a stop beneath the piñon by the side of the house. She always parked in the same spot. Just like she always sought him out whenever she'd been away from the ranch for one hour or several. Her living here as his wife was better than Harlan could have ever imagined. And that was the thing that was scaring the hell out of him.

Recapping the bottle of linseed oil, he dropped it into a wooden storage box, then picked up the saddle and carried it into the tack room. This time he wasn't going to wait for Rose to come to him.

A few minutes later, he stepped into the kitchen. Grocery sacks littered the table and cabinet counters. Both Emily and Rose were busily putting the food items where they belonged.

"Oh, hi, Daddy!" Emily greeted him cheerfully.

His daughter was like a new person now. She never sulked or sassed, or appeared to be bored. Her appetite had increased twofold and she was finally gaining the weight she desperately needed. She rarely ever sat in front of the TV and she was always eager to help him or Rose with whatever needed to be done.

Harlan knew Rose had brought about the change in Emily. She had a mother now and she was blooming under Rose's gentle guidance.

"Hi, you two," he said to both of them.

Rose shoved the canned peaches onto the top shelf of the cabinet, then turned and hurried over to her husband. "Hi, yourself," she said with a wide smile, then slipping her arms around his neck, she raised herself on tiptoe and kissed his mouth.

She smelled like lilacs and tasted even sweeter. In spite of himself, Harlan gripped the sides of her waist and held her close.

"I see you made it back safe and sound," he murmured.

Nodding, she smiled and wrinkled her nose at him. "And I got you something special, too."

"We went grocery shopping and took the twins," Emily spoke up, then giggled. "Oh, boy, was that an experience! Adam tugged a whole tower of toilet paper over onto the floor. And Anna's diaper leaked all over the front of my dress."

Harlan smiled at his daughter. "Sounds like you've been getting a lesson about babies."

She giggled again. "Yeah! Won't it be wonderful if you and Rose have twins?"

Rose groaned with humor while everything inside Harlan went still. Not until yesterday had Rose gone to the doctor to see about birth control. Before then, they'd made love many times without protection. She could be carrying his child at this very moment. And if that were true, he would never be able to protect his heart. She'd have it on a platter. What had he been thinking?

"I believe it would be easier to start with just one," Rose said laughingly, then glanced slyly up at him. "What do you think, Harlan?"

He tried to look as happy and eager as his daughter and wife. "Oh, I think one would definitely be easier to deal with."

Pulling out of Rose's embrace, he went over to the table and peeked inside the grocery bags left on the table. "Did you buy anything sweet?"

Tsking her tongue, Rose pulled the sack away from him before he could dig into it. "Oh, no. Dessert is going to be a surprise. So you just go on and do whatever you were doing and I'll call you when Emily and I have supper ready.''

She nudged him toward the back door, so Harlan complied with her wishes.

Go back to doing what he'd been doing, he thought glumly, as he stepped onto the back porch. He'd been thinking about her. He was always thinking about her. She was the only thing he wanted to think about. So what was he going to do?

Rose made pot roast for supper along with new red potatoes cooked in their jackets, creamed sweet peas and cabbage slaw. But it was the dessert she was proud of. As she placed the huge strawberry shortcake in the middle of the table, Emily oohed and aahed.

"Oh, wow, Rose, that looks delicious. And it's Daddy's favorite, isn't it?" Emily glanced across the table to her father.

Harlan looked from the shortcake piled high with sliced strawberries and whipped cream over to Rose. The eager, loving expression on her face made him feel two inches high.

"It is my favorite. Thank you, Rose."

She reached over and curled her hand over his forearm. "You're very welcome," she told him. "I just hope it doesn't taste like cardboard."

Judging from the things she'd already cooked for him these past two weeks, Harlan knew the cake would taste as good as the touch of her hand on his arm. And in that moment as she served him a portion of the dessert, he knew that he wasn't worthy of this woman. She was too good, too kind to be married to a man who was afraid to love her. Really love her. The way she deserved to be.

"Oh, Rose, everything you make is yummy," Emily spoke up. "And, Daddy, she's gonna teach me how to cook! She says it's easy and I'll be able to learn in no time. Isn't that grand?''

His heart clutched as he thought about all the love Rose had given Emily, all that she would give her in the future. If everything stayed the way it was. If nothing took her away from them.

"It's very grand, sweetheart."

Later that night Harlan shrugged off his shirt and sat down on the side of the bed. Rose was in the shower. Singing. She had a soft melodic voice and anyone could tell by the sound of it that she was a happy woman.

Only a few moments passed before she came out of the bathroom wrapped in a big white towel. As soon as she spotted him, a smile lit her face.

"Tired?"

"No."

"Good." She handed him a wide-toothed comb and presented her back to him. "Then you can get the tangles out for me."

She snuggled up close to him and he began to pull the comb gently through her wet hair. The faint scent of jasmine drifted to his nostrils and though he tried to keep his eyes firmly on her hair, they kept drifting to her shoulders, then further down to where the towel gaped open against her back.

Everything inside him wanted to flip her onto her back, toss away the towel and make love to her until they were both too exhausted to think. But he had to forget about that. He had to stop this incessant desire he had for her.

"Have you heard any word from Justine or Roy about the twins' mother?"

"Justine says that from what information Roy gathered in Albuquerque, he thinks she might be headed south. Possibly this way. I can't imagine why, though. You would think she'd want to steer clear of the crime scene. Unless she might be going to try to kidnap the babies away from us.''

"Hmm. Well, maybe she's the one who cut the fence and let the bull out,'' Harlan mused aloud.

Rose twisted her head around to look at him. "Belinda Waller cut the fence! What makes you think such a thing? Why would she?''

"Look, Rose, if the woman was crazy enough to dump two helpless babies on your porch, she's liable to do anything. As for why, we probably won't know that until Roy catches her.''

Rose straightened her head and Harlan went back to combing her hair. The tangles were nearly gone now, but he liked doing this for her, touching her hair and smoothing his hand over the shiny crown. Being near her for any reason was like a gift to him. And he wondered desperately how he could ever keep himself distanced from her.

"Well, I'll truly be glad when that happens. Just knowing she's out there somewhere makes me uneasy.'' She paused, then looked around at him once more. "You know, Emily and I found something odd this morning.''

His hand stopped on her hair. After the incident with the fence and the lost bull, he'd felt uneasy, too. He worried that Rose or Emily or anyone on the Bar M might be a target to someone for some deranged reason. But Rose already had so many worries to deal with, he hadn't wanted to worry her over something that was just a feeling on his part. "What? Something on the Bar M?''

She nodded. "The watering tank in the west pasture. I'm positive I turned the pump off the windmill last week. Today we found the tank running over and the ground around it saturated. I've never been that negligent before, Harlan. But I must have forgotten or turned the valve the wrong way. Whatever the reason, we can't afford to lose precious water in this drought.''

He was still thinking about the windmill when she turned and took the comb from his hand. With a seductive little smile on her lips, she curled her arms around his neck and nudged him back against the mattress. "I think it's time to thank you for combing my hair."

"Rose, I—" His words came to an abrupt halt as the towel fell away and he was faced with the tantalizing sight of her naked breasts. "I want to...talk to you about something."

Drawing on all his willpower, he quickly wrapped the towel back around her before he could change his mind.

Still smiling, Rose eased back into a sitting position on the bed. "Okay, talk if you must. We'll deal with the thank-you, later."

He swallowed. "Well, I...it's about you and me."

Her smile deepened and she ran her fingers through the hair over his ear. "You've made me so very happy, Harlan. Before you, I didn't know what it could be like to be with a man. Live with a man. And to have a daughter, too." Sighing, she trailed her fingers down the side of his cheek. "I know I still have the problems of the ranch, the twins and Belinda Waller, but now that I have you they don't seem nearly as bad."

Dear God, he felt awful. "I'm...glad, Rose. I want you to be happy."

Her eyes adored his face. "Oh, I am, Harlan. And I want you to be happy, too. You are, aren't you?"

He caught her roaming hand and pressed it between both of his. Studying the tips of her fingers, he said, "You're a wonderful wife, Rose. And mother. But I—"

He couldn't go on. He didn't know how. Or even if he wanted to. He'd never been so torn and miserable in his life.

Rose went very still as she waited for him to continue. When he didn't she bent her head to look up at him. "Harlan, is something wrong? Have I done something to upset you?"

All she'd done was love him. Why couldn't he just accept what she offered and be very happy and grateful for it?

"No. I've just been thinking...and I think we should...uh...not..." His eyes full of torment, he looked up at her. "I think it would be better if we...didn't make love anymore. At least for a while," he added in a rush.

First she appeared shocked, then a wounded, ashen look spread over her face. Harlan felt sick to the very core of his being.

"Oh."

Like a cat suddenly facing a growling dog, she eased back away from him with slow, cautious movements.

"Rose," he said with a groan. "Don't look at me like that. The last thing I want to do is hurt you."

Hurt her? Rose had never felt such splintering pain inside her chest. It was like a thousand daggers stabbing her all at once. "I know. I—"

Careful to keep the towel in place now, she scrambled off the bed. Harlan quickly got to his feet, but when he tried to approach her, she backed away from him like a wild, threatened animal.

"You...don't have to...say anything else, Harlan. I...understand. After all, we didn't marry for...for sex or love or anything like that." She snatched up her bathrobe and pulled it on over the towel as though she was afraid or ashamed that he might see her body. "I'm sorry Harlan. I guess...I got a little starry-eyed these past few days. But that's over with now. I...won't be...pestering you anymore."

Pestering him? Dear Lord, was that what she thought her

lovemaking did to him? No matter what happened he couldn't bear for Rose to think such a thing.

"Rose, don't be—"

Keeping a guarded eye on him, she edged toward the bathroom door. "You know...I don't know what I was thinking. I took a shower, but forgot to wash my feet." She tried to laugh, but it came out more like a choking sob. "I'd better go do that. I wouldn't want to get the sheets dirty."

"Rose!"

He reached for her, but she rushed past him and into the bathroom. Seconds after the door slammed, water was running in the tub. Harlan knew she was in there crying and the fact made him physically ill. But he also knew if he went in there now, if he touched her, all of what he'd just said to her would be for naught.

Harlan was in bed with the lights off when Rose finally came out of the bathroom. Pretending sleep, he listened to the closet door opening and closing, then the soft sound of her footsteps approaching the bed. His stomach clenched like an iron fist as she lifted the covers.

Moments later, he felt something pressing against his back and legs.

"What's this?" He turned over to see her wedging a length of rolled quilt between them.

"Just a reminder," she said quietly, then lay down with her back to him and pulled the sheet up over her shoulder. "Good night, Harlan."

"Good night."

For a long time Harlan stared at her back and the tangled red waves of her hair lying on the pillow. And it dawned on him that he'd done more than put distance between their bodies. From now on she would be apart from him in every way.

What the hell was the matter with him?

* * *

The next morning, when Rose and Emily arrived at the Bar M to work, neither of them were prepared for the scene they found at the stable.

Roy and Randall, his deputy, were searching the building and surrounding area. The stalls were full of mud and water. The horses were running loose in the valley below. Chloe was in furious tears.

Rose and Emily found Chloe sitting in the open doorway of the feed room. Her chin was resting on her fist and her bleary eyes were shooting daggers. She looked ready to kill. "What in the world has happened?" Rose asked.

"We don't know. Someone came in here last night, let the horses out of their stalls, then turned on every hydrant in the place. Oh, and one of my best riding saddles is gone."

"Gee, water is already scarce around here. And it's dangerous for the horses to be running loose like that," Emily spoke up. "Just a little cut from a cactus thorn could mess up a racehorse."

Smiling wanly, Chloe reached up and patted the girl's shoulder. "You're so right, honey. And I know I should be down there trying to gather the horses. But I knew it wouldn't do much good until I got some help."

Roy entered the stable at the opposite end of the building. Rose left the two women and went to speak with him.

"I would say good morning," he said to Rose. "But this mess is hardly good."

"Hi, Roy. Do you have any idea what's happening around here?"

He looked grim as he snapped a small notebook shut and dropped it into his shirt pocket. "There's no question about it, Rose. Someone is out to harm this ranch and consequently our family."

After what Harlan had done to her last night, this was the last thing she needed to hear. But surprisingly, she wasn't feeling much at all. She was dead inside and she was glad. She didn't want to have to worry or think or feel anything anymore.

"Harlan thinks Belinda Waller might have cut the fence. Do you think she could have done this?"

Roy took off his hat and ran his fingers through his sandy hair. He looked tired and angry and Rose realized that he was just as hurt by this as she or her sisters. He truly loved Justine and all of her family. No doubt it was weighing heavily on Roy because he hadn't yet been able to catch Belinda.

"A sheriff doesn't like to speculate, Rose. He'd rather go on the facts he has laying on the table. But to you, I'll say, hell, yes, she's done this. Or if not her, she hired some gunslinger to do it for her. There's no guard dog here and I'm sure that once Chloe and Kitty are asleep they're too tired to be woken up by faint noises."

"I should have left Amos here. But I'm the only one he'll obey, so I figured it would make more sense to let him stay on the Flying H," Rose said with regret. "He might have barked."

"I doubt it. He's a cowdog, not a watchdog. Besides, whoever did this might have fed him a tranquilizer or even poison."

Rose shuddered at the evil thought.

Roy motioned for her to follow him. Once they reached Chloe and Emily, he said, "Look, you three, I don't know exactly what's going on here yet. But I want you all to be very careful. Keep an eye out for anything unusual and don't any of you go riding off alone. Not close to the ranch or far off."

"Don't you think you're going a little bit overboard?" Chloe asked him. "I figure this was meant to be more of a prank than a threat."

Roy shook his head. "The person or persons who did

this wants to deal you some misery. Next time they might not stop at damaging or stealing property."

"You're scaring me," Chloe said, rubbing at the goose bumps on her upper arms.

"Me, too," Emily added. "It gives me the creeps to think someone was sneaking around here."

"Good," Roy said. "I want you all to be spooked enough to be cautious." He arched a brow at Rose, who had so far remained silent. "This means you, too, Rose. If you have to go line riding or checking your cows, I want you to carry a .30-30 with you."

Chloe and Emily gasped at the same time. Rose's wooden expression didn't alter.

"I will," she promised her brother-in-law. But she could have told him she wasn't the least bit afraid for herself. If someone tried to harm her, then so be it. Emily and Chloe were her only concern now.

After Roy and Randall left the ranch to answer another call, Chloe sent Emily to gather up as many lead ropes as she could find to use on the scattered horses. Then she said to Rose, "We need Harlan to help us gather the horses. Will you run up to the house and call him or shall I send Emily?"

"No."

The one word came out short and clipped. Chloe's eyebrows shot up. "No? Rose, what the hell is the matter with you? We need his help."

"He has things of his own to do."

"I can appreciate that. But this is an emergency."

Rose looked past Chloe's shoulder to the soggy, empty stalls. "We can deal with it without him." From now on, she was going to deal with everything without him, she promised herself.

Chloe grabbed her sister's shoulder and hissed sharply, "I don't know what's come over you, but now isn't the time for you to be acting like an ass. You heard Roy. Someone is out to harm us! Some of the horses may already be cut or crippled. We need Harlan's help!''

Rose had needed him, all right. Every fiber of her heart and soul had needed him. He'd known that—she'd shown him so in a thousand ways—yet he'd chosen to turn away from her. He'd taken the most intimate part of her and then decided he didn't want it.

Once again she'd been duped by a man. But this time it was a thousand times worse. Peter might have hurt her body, but Harlan's rejection had been like a knife in the heart.

Rose realized she wasn't nearly as numb as she'd first thought. Tears were brimming over the lids of her eyes and spilling onto her cheeks. ''I…I'm sorry, Chloe. I know I'm behaving badly. I…'' She quickly dashed the tears from her face and glanced around to make sure Emily wasn't within earshot.

''What is it? Has something happened with you and Harlan?'' Chloe guided her sister over to a bale of alfalfa and pushed her down on it. ''Why didn't you tell me this earlier?''

Rose let out a mocking laugh. ''When? I drove up and found another disaster.''

''So what is it? You had a fight? Rose, I'm sure—''

''No. No fight.''

''Then what?''

Rose dropped her head. ''I haven't been completely honest with you about my marriage to Harlan,'' she said, then glumly added, ''or honest with myself either.''

''What do you mean? You told me you loved Harlan. You still do, don't you?''

''I love him desperately,'' she said in a low, strangled voice. ''But…Harlan doesn't love me. He only married me to give Emily a mother.''

"Oh, no, Rose! That can't be true."

She lifted her head as acid tears began to burn her eyes. "It's very true."

Shaking her head, Chloe threw up her hands. "I don't care what you say, I can see for myself when the two of you are together. Harlan adores you. He'd do anything for you."

Except make love to her, Rose thought sickly. She was too awkward and inexperienced, too inept as a woman to please her husband. Of course, she'd feared that very thing from the very beginning. But like a fool, she'd let her runaway feelings for him sway her into his arms. Now she was paying the price.

The whole thing truly was her fault. She'd known she wasn't cut out to be a lover. She shouldn't have ever tried. But when Harlan had kissed her, held her, made love to her, he'd made it seem like he really cared.

Gritting her teeth against the pain, she said, "That's all just an act, Chloe."

Chloe flat out cursed. "Rose, if Harlan is acting he might as well head on up to Broadway. He'd make a darn sight more money there than he would raising cattle." Taking Rose by the shoulder, she nudged her in the direction of the house. "Now dry your eyes and go call him."

Rose lifted the hem of her gingham shirt and dabbed the moisture from her eyes. "You're a hard woman, Chloe."

In spite of the chaos around them, Chloe laughed. "I don't know about hard. But I do know I'm right about you and Harlan. He might have wanted a mother for Emily, but he also wanted you for himself."

Rose knew better, but there wasn't any point in trying to make Chloe understand. After all, what did it matter now? She'd agreed to be a wife of convenience for Harlan. That was her lot in life and she might as well get used to it.

* * *

The night was still hot as Harlan left the horsepen and walked toward the house. His steps were slow and weary, matching the laden beat of his heart. It seemed incredible to him that only a few days ago he'd been a relatively happy man. How had his life gone from bliss to agony in the matter of a few moments?

As he stepped onto the porch he figured Rose was probably getting ready for bed. All of them had put in a long, hot day gathering the horses and mucking out the flooded stalls. She'd more than likely fall to sleep as soon as her head hit the pillow. But he wouldn't. He'd lie awake, wanting to touch her, wanting to hear her soft voice, wanting to pillow her head on his shoulder and feel her hand resting on his chest.

He'd been stupid and reckless to make love to Rose in the first place. But now he was beginning to think he was even more stupid for putting a stop to it.

When he entered the back door, he found Rose sitting at the kitchen table drinking a glass of fruit juice. The moment she spotted him, she clutched the neck of her robe tightly together.

The protective gesture reminded him of how deeply he'd hurt her and he wondered if there was any possible way he could hate himself more.

"I thought you'd be in bed," he said.

Her eyes on the glass in front of her, she shook her head. "It was so hot and dry today I can't seem to get my thirst quenched."

Harlan pulled out the chair across from her. "I wish you didn't have to work so hard, Rose."

She grimaced. "I'm not fragile, Harlan. My name might be Rose, but I'm really a weed."

Maybe she was tenacious, Harlan thought, but even a weed could only take so much before it wilted and died.

"Just the same, I'm not too keen on the idea of you and

Emily riding range tomorrow. If you think that herd of heifers needs to be checked on, then I'll do it.''

"You're sounding like Roy. He made me promise to carry my rifle.''

"Will you?"

She grimaced, then nodded. "Although I don't know why. I couldn't bring myself to shoot a rattlesnake unless it was about to bite Pie or Amos.''

"Even so, you could certainly use it to bluff your way out of trouble.''

She glanced at him and for a moment when their eyes met, Rose felt as if nothing had really changed between them, that if she were to go around the table and kiss his cheek, he wouldn't push her away. But nothing would make her take the chance of having her husband reject her again. She couldn't bear the pain.

"You honestly think there might be trouble?''

"More trouble, you mean?" He nodded grimly. "I don't think this person or persons is through with the Bar M yet. I think they won't be satisfied until it's ruined. Completely.''

Rose suddenly felt cold inside. "It has to be the twins' mother. We have no other enemies.''

"Exactly. And she has to be caught. I'm going to talk to Roy about guarding the ranch house for the next few nights. I could bunk down in the barn and be ready and waiting for anyone who came around.''

And he'd have a good excuse not to go to bed with her, Rose thought painfully. She drained the last of her juice and got up from the table. "I'm not crazy about the idea. But I'm sure you're going to do whatever you want anyway.''

She started out of the kitchen and before Harlan could stop himself he lunged from his chair and snared a hold on her arm.

Rose lifted cool, questioning eyes to his face and he let out a long breath. "I want to say something about last night. I—"

Her spine stiffened and she tugged her arm away from his hold. "I don't want to hear anything about it. There's nothing more to be said, anyway."

He groaned. "Yes. There is. You don't understand why—"

"That's where you're wrong, Harlan. I understand perfectly. You don't love me. And…that's all right. Love wasn't a part of our bargain."

"But I—"

"You thought you could handle a physical relationship with me. You probably even thought you wanted that between us. But then you found out you didn't. Well, that's all right, too. We married for practical reasons and I can live with that. So don't look so miserable. I don't hate you."

She had every right to hate him, Harlan thought. "But I've hurt you and—"

"Like I told you, I'm a weed. You can step on them and even grind them into the dirt with your bootheel, but they somehow survive. So quit worrying. Everything is fine. Just the way you wanted it."

She was either one hell of an actress or he'd managed to kill what love she'd had for him. He should be relieved. But he wasn't. Everything inside him ached and all he really wanted to do was pull her into his arms and never let her go.

"Good night, Harlan." Her head up, her shoulders straight, she walked away from him before he could see the tears on her cheeks.

"Do you think Emily needs to go to the doctor? Maybe she got a touch of sunstroke yesterday," Harlan said to

Rose the next morning as she climbed into the cab of her truck.

Rose shook her head. "I think she's just tired. If she doesn't feel any better by tonight, I'll have Justine come take a look at her."

Rose shut the door. Harlan stepped up and rested both his hands on the open window. "This isn't like her. She always wants to do everything with you. Do you think she's afraid to go back to the Bar M?"

When he was close to her like this, Rose couldn't make her eyes stay anywhere else but on him. Even though it hurt to look into his face, meet his warm brown eyes and pretend she didn't love him.

"No," she answered. "Even if Emily was afraid, she's not a coward. She'd go with me come hell or high water."

Unlike her father, Harlan thought ruefully. If he had real courage he'd haul Rose out of the truck and show her just how much he wanted to make love to her. And damn the fear of losing her. But he knew what it was like to love someone, then lose them. He couldn't forget the weeks and months he'd lived in a black haze, the pain he'd endured trying to struggle out of it. How could he let himself love like that again? Feel that much again?

Once Rose had driven away, Harlan went back into the house to check on Emily. He found her already out of bed and dressed in jeans and a long-sleeved shirt. She was hopping on one foot while tugging a cowboy boot onto the other.

"What are you doing, honey? I thought you told Rose you didn't feel like getting up this morning."

Her expression a bit sheepish, she said, "I know. I sorta lied about that. But I had good reason."

Her boots on, she picked up a hairbrush and began to tug it through her hair. Harlan walked further into the room.

"Okay, Emily," he said firmly. "I want to know what

is going on. Are you angry at Rose? Why didn't you want to go with her this morning? You're obviously not sick.''

Emily whipped a rubberband around the tail of her hair, then turned to face her father. In that moment he realized more than ever how she was growing into a young adult.

"I did want to go with her. But I wanted to talk to you. Alone. Without Rose here. So I figured this was the best way to do it.''

Harlan stared at his daughter. "You must be very unhappy about something to go to this much trouble to get my attention. Does this involve Rose?''

She nodded emphatically, then went over and flopped down on the edge of the bed. The mattress bounced beneath her.

"I guess I'm just confused about a lot of things," she said, then propping both elbows on her knees, she rested her chin in her hands.

"About what?''

She frowned at him. "Daddy, do you love me?''

He chuckled fondly. "Of course I love you. I tell you so, don't I?''

She continued to frown at him. "Yes. But do you love me enough to do almost anything for me?''

He shrugged as he tried to figure out where her young thinking was headed. For the life of him, he couldn't figure what was prompting Emily's odd behavior this morning. "Well, anything within reason.''

"Enough to marry Rose?''

He went very still and then he saw it on her face. A strange mix of accusation and hurt and anger roiling just beneath the surface.

"What do you mean? Has someone been saying things? Has Rose said—''

"No one has been saying anything to me!'' she interrupted. "All I want to know, Daddy, is why did you marry Rose? Just so I could have a mother?"

How very different, how simple it all seemed now that Emily had put the question out loud to him. Why hadn't he seen it before? Why had he kept trying to make his marriage to Rose into anything but what it really was? A union of love.

Because he'd been so afraid of losing her that he'd been blinded to what had already happened. He was in love with Rose. He had been from the very start.

When Harlan failed to answer, Emily prompted, "Surely that can't be so hard to answer, Daddy."

Harlan went over and sat down next to her. "It isn't hard to answer, honey," he said gently. "But first of all I want to know why you're asking all of this?"

She looked at him with worried blue eyes. "Because I can tell something is wrong. And yesterday Rose was crying and I overheard her tell Chloe that you didn't love her, that you only married her so that I could have a mother."

Pain splintered inside his chest. "I wish you hadn't heard that, Emily. Because it isn't true."

Her eyes widened. "Rose doesn't lie!"

A wan smile touched Harlan's lips. "No. Rose doesn't lie. She was upset. She doesn't understand that I do love her. Very much."

Emily let out a long breath, then gave her father a big smile. "That's what I thought. So maybe you'd better tell her and make her understand. I can't bear to see her unhappy."

The pain in his chest was gone now, replaced with the elated contentment of finally knowing what was in his heart.

"Oh, my little darling," he said, curling one arm around her shoulders and hugging her to him. "I think you are very, very right. What do you say me and you drive on over to the Bar M, so I can find your new mom and tell her just that?''

Emily jumped up from the bed and crammed her hat on her head. ''I say I'm ready! Oh, and Daddy,'' she added as the two of them left the bedroom, ''Let's just tell Rose I got to feeling better real fast.''

Harlan laughed. ''All right. But no more faking.''

Emily made a crisscross on her chest. ''Cross my heart.''

And no more faking for him either, Harlan promised himself.

When Harlan and Emily arrived at the Bar M, Rose had already ridden off on Pie to check the heifers. Deciding he wasn't going to waste any more time, Harlan went down to the stable and saddled one of the working horses. He was going to find Rose and tell her exactly how he felt about her. Maybe she wouldn't believe him. Maybe he'd already hurt her so badly she wouldn't care. In any case, he had to try to make things right.

Forty-five minutes later, Harlan spotted her. She was sitting on a rock beneath a ragged stand of mesquite trees. As he climbed down from his mount, she stared at him as if he were the last person on earth she expected to see. Then her expression quickly turned to near panic. ''What's the matter? Has Emily gotten sick? Is Justine—''

Harlan shook his head as he looped his horse's reins over a nearby tree branch. ''Nothing is wrong. Nothing that can't be righted, I hope.''

She eyed him warily as he walked toward her. ''Something has happened!''

She started to rise to her feet, but by then Harlan was there to put a hand on her shoulder and push her back on the rock.

''I came looking for you because we need to talk,'' he told her.

Dear God, he wasn't going to put her through that humiliation again, was he? If that was his intention, she'd get on Pie and ride till he couldn't find her.

"Harlan, please...I don't want to rehash anything about...our marriage. You either want to stay married, or you don't. Which is it?"

Suddenly he was laughing in a way that Rose had never seen before. His eyes were sparkling and the sound coming from deep inside him was so warm and infectious that she very nearly wanted to smile herself. And she would have if her heart wasn't so full of pain.

"My darling Rosie, do you really have to ask that? Of course I want to stay married to you."

Of course, he says. As though she was the love, the very light of his life. Who was he trying to kid? she wondered.

Sinking down on the ground beside her, Harlan reached for her hand and drew the back of it to his lips. Bemused, Rose stared at him.

"Last night you said you didn't hate me. Is that true?" he asked.

Over his right shoulder, she could see the heifers pilfering among the sagebrush for a blade or two of grama grass. The cows were as hungry as her heart, she realized. But the cows could and would be fed, even if she had to haul alfalfa out here to do it. Her heart, well, that was another matter.

"Yes. It was true. How could I hate you? You've done so much for me."

He pressed his lips to her hand once more and Rose could only wonder how such a little kiss could make her shiver in a hundred degree heat.

"Then you do love me?"

Her eyes flew to his face. "Love you?"

He nodded gravely. "I thought you loved me after we got married. Do you still?"

She couldn't look at him as pain began to fill her chest.

"Why are you asking? So you can tell me I'll have to quit doing that, too?"

Rose didn't get the answer she was expecting. Before she realized his intentions Harlan pulled her off the rock and onto his lap.

"What are you doing?" she demanded, then gasped as he tilted her head against the crook of his arm.

"I'm trying to get an answer out of you. Now tell me truthfully. It's very important."

She couldn't be in his arms like this and lie to him. Even to save her own pride. "Yes. I love you, Harlan."

He closed his eyes, then crushed her tightly against his chest. Stunned by it all, Rose simply clung to him and thanked God that for these few moments, at least, he wanted her.

"Oh, Rose," he said with a groan, then eased her far enough away to reach her face. He rained little kisses over her forehead, cheeks, nose and finally her lips. "Rosie, I don't deserve you, you know. But I'm so very grateful I have you."

Still totally bewildered by this sudden change in him, Rose stared up at his face. "I don't understand, Harlan. I thought you—"

He placed a fingertip against her lips. "I was a fool, Rose. I've been a fool for a long time now."

"And what made you decide this?" she had to ask.

"Emily opened my eyes. She wanted to know why I married you."

Rose's heart suddenly forgot to beat. "I hope you didn't tell her the truth. She'd be hurt. She thinks we're a real family."

Harlan's head swung back and forth. "I did tell her the truth. I told her I loved you. And I do. I expect I fell in love with you that first night you walked up to my horsepen and said hello."

She struggled to get out of his lap, but he refused to let her go. "Harlan, it isn't necessary for you to say any of this. I told you last night I understand—"

"You couldn't, Rose! Until this morning I didn't understand it myself. All this time I've been telling myself I wanted you to be my wife because Emily needed you, that the house needed a woman's touch, that you needed my help with the ranch. But none of those things is the real reason I married you. I wanted you to be my wife because I love you. And I want you with me for always."

She'd made the mistake of thinking he cared for her once. How could she be reckless enough to do it twice? "Harlan, I know you're trying to be kind to me, but—"

Before she could get another word out, his arm tightened around her, his head swooped down to hers. "Kind, hell! Right now, I'm feeling anything but kind, Rose."

Her heart began to pound with wild, sweet hope as his lips nibbled hungrily at her throat. "You said you'd never let yourself love another woman," she said pointedly.

"Hmm. Well, I wasn't nearly as strong as I thought." He pulled the scarf from her ponytail and ran his fingers through the long red waves. "Like an idiot, I believed I could make love to you and keep my heart out of it. But it didn't work that way."

"You said you didn't want to make love to me anymore," she whispered, the pain of that moment mirrored in her eyes. "Do you know how much that hurt me?"

His features twisted with anguish. "You can't imagine how much it hurt me. But I was crazy, Rose. Crazy with fear. Each time we made love I knew I was falling that much harder for you. And it scared me. All I could think about was loving you and then losing you...the way I lost Karen."

Rose's heart was suddenly aching with the need to reassure him. "Oh, Harlan, none of us knows what tomorrow might bring. That's why we have to take what we have today. Love each other today and be happy for it.''

"I remember a time not so long ago that you didn't feel that way. You were afraid to marry me.''

She reached up and touched his face, then smiled with the sheer joy of knowing her husband loved her. "I'm not sure I wasn't afraid ten minutes ago. But I'm not now. Now that I know you love me.''

Groaning deep in his throat, he buried his face in her hair. "I couldn't stand you being distant with me. I couldn't bear not making love to you.''

Suddenly his fingers were on the buttons of her blouse and Rose laughed softly as the fabric quickly parted and his lips found the valley between her breasts.

"Harlan! We're out here in the pasture! Anyone might come along!''

Chuckling, he continued to unbutton her clothing. "You and Emily are the only one's who've ridden across this land in months and she's back at the ranch baby-sitting the twins. So we're all alone. And I've got a fever only you can cure.''

Put like that, Rose didn't care if they were out in the middle of nowhere beneath a few ragged mesquite trees. She'd never felt this much happiness in her life, never had her heart so filled to the brim with love.

With a sly little smile, she pulled the stampede string over her head, then tossed her hat out of the way. "Okay, Mr. Hamilton, I'm ready to see if you can back up all this talk.''

Growling with laughter, he flipped her onto the ground, then hunkered over her on his hands and knees. "In a few minutes I'm gonna have you thinking you're in heaven.''

Grabbing the front of his shirt, Rose pulled him down against the length of her. "That's a pretty tall order, cowboy. You think you can fill it?''

Love shone on his face as he lowered his head to hers. Rose wound her arms around his neck and gave herself up to the hungry demand of his mouth.

So lost was she in his kiss, it took her several moments to smell the smoke. When she did, she pushed at Harlan's shoulders and struggled to sit up.

"Harlan, something is on fire!"

He grinned at her mussed hair and swollen lips. "I thought it was you and me."

"No! Something is burning! Smell the smoke?"

Seeing she was serious, Harlan lifted his head and sniffed. Then he saw it, a gray-white cloud of smoke rising to the south of them.

"Something *is* burning." He stood up for a better look. Rose scrambled to her feet and grabbed her hat.

"Can you tell where it is?" she asked shading her eyes with her hand and peering in the general direction of the smoke.

"It's on Bar M land," he said grimly.

Fear shot through Rose. "Dear God, it's not the house, is it?"

She was shaking so badly, her fingers refused to work. Seeing her distress, Harlan brushed her hands aside and buttoned her shirt.

"No. The smoke is south of here and the house. Maybe we'd better mount up and see what's going on."

Nodding, she crammed on her hat and drew the stampede string tight beneath her chin.

"I'm ready!"

Harlan handed her Pie's reins then gathered his own mount. In moments they were riding into the wind and open range. In less than five minutes they reached a small summit where they reined the horses to an abrupt halt. Beyond them, no more than a hundred yards away a wall of fire spanned at least a mile or more.

"Oh…oh, Harlan, it's a sea of fire!" Rose shouted. "What are we going to do?"

"There's nothing we can do to stop it, Rose. I'd say we better hightail it back to the house and call the firefighters. If we're lucky, Chloe or someone has already spotted the smoke and put in the call."

Rose nodded in agreement and they turned their horses and urged them into a desperate gallop back along the trail they'd taken only moments earlier.

They had ridden a half mile when Harlan shouted for her attention, then pointed to the left of him. Rose's stomach nosedived with terror as she saw another wall of fire sweeping straight at them.

"We can't outrun that! Not in this heat and wind!" Pie was already lathered and heaving with exhaustion. She wasn't going to kill her horse just to try and save herself. She couldn't.

"I'd already decided that. Come on! If I remember right, there's an arroyo somewhere east of here. We'll ride to the bottom of it and hope the fire jumps over us."

Rose followed his lead while telling herself not to panic. Fire couldn't move that fast, could it? But each time she glanced over her shoulder, she could see the flames were gaining ground on the two of them. Fanned by the wind, smoke and burning sparks soon enveloped the whole area. Rose reined Pie abreast of Harlan's mount and reached for his hand. He squeezed it tightly and yelled over the din of the flames.

"Don't worry, we're almost there!"

"But the fire is almost on us!" Even as she spoke pieces of burning sage and piñon whipped around their heads.

"We'll be all right. Trust me!"

It seemed like ages passed before they finally reached the arroyo and scrambled to the bottom of it. Harlan shoved

Rose into the first crevice he could find, then stripped off his heavy denim shirt and covered the both of them.

Sweat was streaming between their faces and Rose wasn't sure which was louder, her heart pounding in her ears or the roar of the fire.

"Don't be scared, my Rosie. I'm not going to let anything happen to you," Harlan said against her ear.

Rose was gripping his shoulder so tightly her fingers ached. "This is crazy. You finally decide you want to be a real husband to me and now we're both going to be fried!"

In spite of the approaching danger, Harlan's chest shook with laughter. "I didn't know you had a sense of humor, Rose. I got a real deal when I talked you into marrying me."

"Sure! I'm going to get you killed!"

Smoke had found their little hole in the bluff. Rose tried not to cough, but after a few moments it was impossible not to. Burying her face in Harlan's neck, she held her breath for as long as she could and prayed the fire would miss them.

"Just keep holding onto me," Harlan whispered. "It'll be over us soon."

He was right. In only a matter of moments, the roar and the intense heat was gone. Slowly, Harlan uncovered them and helped Rose to her feet. Her legs were so weak, she was forced to hold on to his waist to steady herself.

"If it keeps heading the way it's going it should stop when it hits the river," he said.

Shocked by the sight around her, Rose whispered in a stricken voice. "Everything is black!"

"Yes, but at least we're safe."

Through bleary eyes, she smiled at his soot- and dirt-streaked face. "And we're together. That's all that matters to me, Harlan."

Pulling her tight against him, he let his kiss tell her just how grateful he was for her and her love.

"Do you think you can ride now?"

Nodding, she let him lead her over to Pie, who seemed none the worse for wear other than black soot marks on his legs and shoulders. Harlan's mount appeared to be equally sound and Rose found it incredible that the four of them had narrowly escaped being burned.

A half hour later they reached the ranch yard. Emily came racing out to meet them. Tears of relief poured down her face as she flung herself first at her father, then at Rose.

"We were afraid you'd been burned! We were about to ride out on the horses to look for you!"

"We're fine, honey. Just a little hot and dirty," Harlan assured her. "Is everyone here okay?"

Emily nodded. "The fire didn't come this way, thank goodness."

By now Roy and Chloe had joined them and for the next few moments it was chaos as everyone tried to talk at once.

"You two look awful!" Chloe exclaimed.

Rose glanced at Harlan and then herself. They were both covered with dirt, soot and sweat. But in her eyes Harlan had never looked better. And the way he kept smiling at her, she'd never felt more beautiful.

"Most of the flash fire has burned itself out," Roy exclaimed, "but the firefighters are dealing with what's still smoldering north of here."

"I only hope there weren't many cattle lost," Harlan told him. "Do you have any idea where the fire started? Rose and I saw the smoke and went to check on it, but by the time we found the flames, the whole range looked like it was on fire."

Roy and Chloe exchanged grim glances while Emily practically bounced on her toes.

"Roy caught her!" Emily burst out excitedly. "He

caught Belinda Waller after she set the fires! And he found jugs of gas and matches in the back of her car!''

Rose and Harlan stared at each other then at Roy. "Is this true?" Rose asked. "She set the fires?"

Roy nodded. "We got a tip from a service station where she purchased several jugs of gas. The attendant thought she was acting strangely and needed to be checked out. The description he gave us vaguely matched Belinda's, so on a hunch I headed out here to the ranch. Unfortunately, she'd already set the fires before Randall and I could head her off.''

The shock of it all left Rose sagging weakly against Harlan. Both his arms came around her waist to support her. "But how...why did she want to kill us?" Rose murmured.

Roy shook his head. "I don't really think the woman was out to kill anyone. I doubt she knew either of you would be anywhere near the fires. But she did admit she wanted to destroy the ranch and everything you girls owned.''

"But why?" she asked in bewilderment. "What did we ever do to the woman?"

"Maybe we'll know more later when we can question her more extensively. But when we first picked her up she was pretty much out of it. She kept rambling about Tomas's daughters having everything while she had nothing. From what I can gather, it appears to be a simple case of revenge. If she couldn't have Tomas and the ranch, then she didn't want you daughters having it either.''

"You say she was out of it," Harlan spoke. "Do you mean drunk on something or just crazy?"

"We found several prescription drugs in her handbag, none of which we think were obtained legally. From the looks of her, she's had a drug problem for some time now."

Rose shook her head with sick regret. Chloe said,

"What's even worse, she didn't even ask about her babies."

Rose looked at her brother-in-law. She knew he'd been working practically night and day trying to track down Adam and Anna's mother. If anything, she was relieved for his sake that he'd finally captured the woman. "Did you question her about the twins?"

Roy nodded. "She says she left them with Tomas. He wanted them. She didn't."

Stunned, Rose said, "Oh my Lord. Did she not know Daddy was dead?"

"I don't think so," Roy answered ruefully. "When we told her, she accused us of lying. At this point, I think she's too mentally unstable to comprehend much of anything."

"Does that mean she could get out of jail on an insanity plea?" Chloe asked in outrage.

Knowing his young sister-in-law's quick temper, Roy held up a calming hand. "Don't worry, Chloe. Belinda Waller has done too much to be let loose on society again. I assure you she'll be locked up in some sort of facility, whether it be for the criminally insane or not."

Later that night after things had settled down enough for the three of them to go home to the Flying H, Rose and Harlan sat on the front porch as lightning danced across the western sky.

Her head pillowed against Harlan's shoulder, Rose said drowsily, "It would rain now, after half of the Bar M is burned to a crisp."

"I know, it would be ironic," Harlan replied. "But it would be wonderful just the same. With a little water on the ground, the grass will sprout back quickly and save us a big feed bill."

She sighed with contentment. "Well, frankly, I'm glad we've had this drought."

He lifted her head away from him. "Woman, are you crazy? This has been a hell of a summer!"

She smiled at his outrage. "I know. But the drought brought us together. Otherwise, we might have simply gone on being neighbors. Now look at us. We're married."

His eyes warm with love, he drew her head back against his shoulder. "Yeah. And in love."

"I know we lost a few cows in the fire. And I know it's going to be a long struggle before the ranch gets out of the red again, but I can't imagine being any happier than I am at this moment." She twisted her head up to give him a smile. "Well, I might be a bit happier once I know that Chloe has the twins safely adopted in her name. She wants those babies so badly. She needs them, in fact."

Harlan gently rubbed her arm as wind from the coming rain began to cool the porch. "And they need her. She'll be a good, devoted mother. I think Chloe's dream will come true once Belinda has come to trial and a judge weighs all the facts."

"You know, I keep thinking about something Roy told us," Rose mused aloud. "When he asked Belinda about the babies, she said that Tomas wanted them. She didn't. I wonder what that meant?"

He sighed. "I don't know, Rosie. But I can tell you one thing, Tomas might have liked to gamble and drink his bourbon at times, but that didn't mean he wasn't a good man at heart. I know he loved children and he must have wanted those babies. I understand what he did wasn't right. But when a man knows he's losing his wife, the woman he loves, it makes him do crazy things. Look at me. I tried to drive a wall between us. I didn't want to let you get close just because I was afraid of going through that sort of pain again."

Without saying a word, she lifted her head and planted a kiss on his cheek. He cupped his hand along the side of her face. "Rose, you remember those birth-control pills you got from the doctor the other day?"

She nodded. "What about them?"

"I want you to throw them away."

She twisted around to face him. "Have you had heat-stroke? Harlan, those things cost a fortune!"

He threw back his head and laughed. "Oh, my practical Rose. Forget about what the damn things cost! I want us to have a baby."

"A baby?" She breathed the word as though he'd just taken her to a sacred place. "When did you decide this?"

He grinned as he ran his fingers through her silky red hair. "I think I decided it the moment you said we have to love each other today and be happy for it."

For an answer Rose flung her arms around his neck and placed a warm, promising kiss on his mouth.

His heart too full to say a word, Harlan lifted his wife in his arms and carried her inside to their bed.

Outside, the rain began to fall.

*   *   *   *   *

And the Winner Is...
You!

...when you pick up these great titles
from our new promotion at your
favorite retail outlet this June!

Diana Palmer
The Case of the Mesmerizing Boss

Betty Neels
The Convenient Wife

Annette Broadrick
Irresistible

Emma Darcy
A Wedding to Remember

Rachel Lee
Lost Warriors

Marie Ferrarella
Father Goose

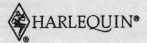 

twins
on the doorstep
by Stella Bagwell

When the Murdock sisters found abandoned twins
on their ranch-house doorstep, they had no clue the
little ones would lead them to love!

Come see how each sister meets her match—and how
the twins' family is discovered—in

THE SHERIFF'S SON (SR #1218, April 1997)

THE RANCHER'S BRIDE (SR #1224, May 1997)

THE TYCOON'S TOTS (SR #1228, June 1997)

TWINS ON THE DOORSTEP—a brand-new miniseries
by Stella Bagwell starting in April…
Only from

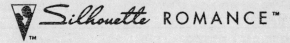

Silhouette ROMANCE™

As seen on TV!
Free Gift Offer

With a Free Gift proof-of-purchase from any Silhouette® book,
you can receive a beautiful cubic zirconia pendant.

This gorgeous marquise-shaped stone is a genuine cubic
zirconia—accented by an 18" gold tone necklace.

(Approximate retail value $19.95)

Send for yours today...
compliments of **Silhouette®**

To receive your free gift, a cubic zirconia pendant, send us one original proof-of-
purchase, photocopies not accepted, from the back of any Silhouette Romance™,
Silhouette Desire®, Silhouette Special Edition®, Silhouette Intimate Moments®
or Silhouette Yours Truly™ title available in February, March and April at your favorite
retail outlet, together with the Free Gift Certificate, plus a check or money order for
$1.65 U.S./$2.15 CAN. (do not send cash) to cover postage and handling, payable
to Silhouette Free Gift Offer. We will send you the specified gift. Allow 6 to 8 weeks for
delivery. Offer good until April 30, 1997 or while quantities last. Offer valid in the
U.S. and Canada only.

Free Gift Certificate

Name: _____

Address: _____

City: _____ State/Province: _____ Zip/Postal Code: _____

Mail this certificate, one proof-of-purchase and a check or money order for postage
and handling to: SILHOUETTE FREE GIFT OFFER 1997. In the U.S.: 3010 Walden
Avenue, P.O. Box 9077, Buffalo NY 14269-9077. In Canada: P.O. Box 613, Fort Erie,
Ontario L2Z 5X3.

FREE GIFT OFFER   084-KFD
ONE PROOF-OF-PURCHASE
To collect your fabulous FREE GIFT, a cubic zirconia pendant, you must include this
original proof-of-purchase for each gift with the properly completed Free Gift Certificate.

084-KFD

IT'S A MONTH OF WEDDED BLISS!

In July, Silhouette Romance is proud to present six irresistible novels about love and marriage. Don't miss:

#1234 *And Baby Makes Six* by Pamela Dalton
It's A Girl!

#1235 *Three Kids And A Cowboy* by Natalie Patrick
Second Chance At Marriage

#1236 *Just Say I Do* by Lauryn Chandler
Substitute Groom

#1237 *The Bewildered Wife* by Vivian Leiber
The Bride Has Amnesia!

#1238 *Have Honeymoon, Need Husband* by Robin Wells
Runaway Bride

#1239 *A Groom for Maggie* by Elizabeth Harbison
Green Card Marriage

Don't miss a single one, available in July, only from

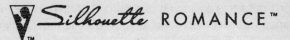

Silhouette ROMANCE™

**This summer, the legend
continues in Jacobsville**

Diana Palmer

A LONG, TALL
TEXAN SUMMER

Three **BRAND-NEW** short stories

This summer, Silhouette brings readers a special
collection for Diana Palmer's LONG, TALL TEXANS
fans. Diana has rounded up three **BRAND-NEW**
stories of love Texas-style, all set in Jacobsville,
Texas. Featuring the men you've grown to love from
this wonderful town, this collection is a must-have
for all fans!

*They grow 'em tall in the saddle in Texas—and
they've got love and marriage on their minds!*

Don't miss this collection of original Long, Tall Texans
stories...available in June at your favorite retail outlet.

LTTST

IN CELEBRATION OF MOTHER'S DAY, JOIN
SILHOUETTE THIS MAY AS WE BRING YOU

a funny thing
HAPPENED ON THE WAY TO THE
Delivery Room

THESE THREE STORIES, CELEBRATING THE
LIGHTER SIDE OF MOTHERHOOD, ARE
WRITTEN BY YOUR FAVORITE AUTHORS:

KASEY MICHAELS
KATHLEEN EAGLE
EMILIE RICHARDS

When three couples make the trip to the delivery
room, they get more than their own bundles of
joy…they get the promise of love!

Available this May,
wherever Silhouette books are sold.

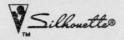
Silhouette®

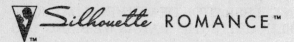
Silhouette ROMANCE™

cordially invites you to the unplanned nuptials
of three unsuspecting hunks and their

SURPRISE BRIDES

Look for the following specially packaged titles:

March 1997: MISSING: ONE BRIDE by Alice Sharpe, #1212
April 1997: LOOK-ALIKE BRIDE by Laura Anthony, #1220
May 1997: THE SECRET GROOM by Myrna Mackenzie, #1225

Don't miss **Surprise Brides,** an irresistible trio of books about love
and marriage by three talented authors! Found only in—

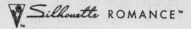
Silhouette ROMANCE™